Last Chance Salon

Last Chance Salon

FJ McNeill

Bridge House

British Library Cataloguing in Publication Data
A Record of this Publication is available from the British
Library

ISBN 978-1-907335-78-5

This edition published 2020 by Bridge House Publishing
Manchester, England

Contents

Last Chance Salon

My trouble is that I'm way too trusting. Always ready to see the good in people. It's got me into hot water more than once, I can tell you.

So when I got talking to a bloke in a pub and he gave me a hard-luck story, I fell for it, hook, line and solid gold sinker. He had a business he needed shot of, he said. His wife was none too well, they were moving abroad, he said.

"I don't suppose you... no, silly question. Forget I mentioned it," he shrugged.

He sighed and looked into the middle distance with eyes that spoke of wisdom and pain endured. The sort of facial expression that looms large in cowboy films. Think Clint Eastwood in a poncho, chewing on a cheroot, or John Wayne on a dusty ranch putting a recalcitrant young'un in his place.

Of course, with all my years of hamming it up, I should have spotted his technique a mile off. No such luck.

"No, no," I urged. "Please go on."

And so I woke up the morning after with a pounding head and the keys to 'Hairs & Graces' in Penge. Penge! I ask you! Even the name sounds like a cross between 'penny-pinching' and 'gunge'. I couldn't have chosen a less glamorous location if I'd tried. I'd been through it once or twice on the way to somewhere else but never had reason to stop. And when I went down there to take a look first-hand at the turkey I'd bought, I very nearly kept on walking.

Hairs & Graces was the three Ds – dismal, dreary and run-down – and sandwiched between a newsagent and a tyre-fitting workshop. The outside was painted a light green, cheap soap colour and it was peeling off in places, lending a scabby look. There were yellowing nets like old ladies' drawers in the window and posters of beehives and sideburns that were so old they'd faded to green in the sunlight.

Inside was no better. I'd been hoping for rough plasterwork, maybe a little chrome here and there, but the place looked as though it hadn't changed since the Fab Four made bowl cuts popular.

The walls were the colour of pink instant pudding and the floor covered in grey lino. The glass tables, the coat rack, even the pot plant holders were embellished with white, curly, wrought iron, all collecting dust. There were even some of those old-fashioned, space helmet-style dryers. It would have taken several thousand pounds to modernise the place and I just didn't have that kind of money. I could have cried.

So I did what I usually do in times of crisis. I put my feet up, lit a fag and considered my options.

What I really wanted was my money back. But even if I went back to the Hope & Anchor, (known locally as the 'Dope & Wanker', which seemed an accurate enough description of me, given the circumstances) to track down Mr Grant P. Worrall, I was unlikely to be successful. I'd signed the papers and he'd disappeared into the sunset.

On the other hand, I could have a bash at running the place, I speculated. I'd spent a few months in the wig department of a regional theatre and could probably manage a trim or a blow-dry. Perms were out of fashion and colouring was just like playing with a chemistry set. The punters round here were unlikely to have high expectations. How hard could it be?

But then again, sound financial acumen had never been my strong point, not that it had ever stopped me from trying. I was a landscape gardener for a while but I wrenched my back pushing a wheelbarrow full of turf. I sold trinkets from the Far East on a market stall until the whole of my stock was pinched from the back of the van.

I even managed a rock band for a year or two. Great fun

but the lead guitarist was hard work. Always bloody complaining. One day he took exception to my socks. As I recall they had a rather nice, pink and grey Argyle pattern and my mother had given them to me for Christmas.

"You're wearing middle class socks," he announced, as if that were the ultimate betrayal, though of what I couldn't tell.

I can't speak for my socks but I'd never made any claims that I was anything other than middle class. I was privately educated. My father played golf. I didn't see what the problem was. But I'd had enough of him and his griping and it was time for something new. So I walked out. Never saw any of them again which was a bit of a shame. Sound lads, the rest of them. Last I heard, they were gigging in a pub off the A2.

However, I'm nothing if not optimistic. Every time I begin some new enterprise I think, "This time, it's going to work. I'll show 'em all that Rafe Bunce can be a success."

But, sitting there in that has-been hair salon, I suddenly felt myself completely spent, like someone had pulled my plug out. I had one of those moments of clarity people often talk about. An epiphany, you might say. Who was I kidding? I wasn't a successful businessman running an empire from a luxury penthouse. I was a chain-smoking, fifty-something, sometime actor in a cardigan, washed-up in a stagnant corner of south London.

Who to turn to but The Bard for a fitting phrase to sum up my anguish? "O, I am fortune's fool!" I wailed, putting my head in my hands.

I heard a noise like someone clearing their throat. I slowly lifted my head and saw a figure silhouetted against the light. My first thought was that the place was haunted. It would have come as no surprise.

I screamed and leapt to my feet.

"Sorry," someone said. "I didn't mean to scare you."

A young woman stepped forward, not yet eighteen years old by my reckoning, and wearing a dark blue raincoat in the style once favoured by district nurses. Her hair was cropped short, her face was freckly and her small, slightly slanting eyes looked much too knowing for her years.

"The door was open," she explained in a voice that sounded different to the usual Penge-ish twang.

Seeing that she was, in fact, a living being who had entered the premises in the standard way rather than wafting through a wall, I composed myself.

"Yes. Well," I said, trying to make my voice a bit deeper. "What can I do for you?"

"I work 'ere," she said.

That took me by surprise. Judging by the amount of mail silted up on the doormat when I'd come in, I'd assumed the salon was no longer functioning.

"Are you sure?" I said.

"Mr Worrall said he was closing for a while. Said I was to keep stopping by to see when it was open again," she went on.

I was certain I wouldn't be able to pay myself, let alone any staff. "I'm the new owner and no-one said anything to me about any employees," I pointed out. "I'm sorry, but…" I let the unspoken assumption that she would have to clear off hang in the air.

"But I'm the junior hairdresser," she answered, pronouncing it 'ur-dresser'. She had a soft voice but there was no mistaking her determination.

It was then than I pinpointed her accent. Lancashire, if I wasn't mistaken. Bolton to be precise. I'd done panto up there one year.

"Well, I'm very sorry but—"

The door opened and someone else came in.

"Hello Suky, love!" said an old lady in a knitted hat that looked like porridge, coming towards the girl. "I'm not late, am I?"

"No, you're fine," she answered. "Take a seat and I'll be with you in a minute."

I had the sense, then, of being elbowed out of the way. Upstaged, as it were, and I didn't like it. I was pretty sure Richard Branson didn't have to put up with this kind of thing.

"Now hang on just one minute," I warned, holding my hand up like a traffic cop and addressing my remarks to the room at large, lest anyone else was lurking in there. "We're not actually open at present."

The old lady stared at me, her lips twitching, as if she didn't understand what I was saying. Suky, as the girl was apparently called, picked up a book from the cash desk and brought it over to me.

"Mrs Abercrombie has a booking," she whispered, pointing at that day's entry.

"Oh. I see. Well, just this once," I huffed. "After that, we're definitely closed. *Definitely*."

Suky changed into an overall, took the woman's coat and set about washing and styling her hair.

I lit another cigarette, reverted to my former boots-up position and observed. The girl appeared to know what she was doing. She was quick and quiet in her movements, her comb darting like a viper's tongue as she spooled the woman's hair onto rollers.

But as I watched, I was struck by the quality of Suky's own hair. It had a texture unlike anything I had ever seen growing out of someone's cranium. It was like shredded wheat, coconut matting or the fuzzy texture inside a suede boot. The poor girl, it had to be said, looked like a boiled sweet that had been hanging around in someone's pocket and had bits of tobacco stuck all over it. Still, she obviously wasn't letting it hold her back.

When Mrs Abercrombie's session was finished, she paid and left the salon smiling. But before Suky could put the cash in the till, I snatched it from her hand.

"There you go," I said, thrusting a tenner at her. "Thank you for your efforts. Now, if you don't mind—"

"We've got three bookings first thing," she said, ignoring the money.

"Three?" I hesitated.

"A restyle, highlights and a set," she nodded.

I wouldn't be able to cope with that lot by myself and she knew it.

"Well, maybe come back just for tomorrow, then," I relented. "But after that we're closed. *Definitely.*"

Suky came back the following morning and the next day and the next day after that. Soon she'd been there three weeks. I was forced to admit to myself that the salon was indeed open for business and what's more, I had an employee.

So, reluctantly, I moved into the flat above with a load of brown, second-hand furniture and tapped my old man for yet another loan in order to meet running costs. Between us Suky and I managed to meet the modest needs of our clientele, she tackling the more elaborate hairstyles, leaving basic washing, setting and trimming to me.

I quite enjoyed myself, truth be known. I was master of my own domain and the old ladies were an appreciative audience for my rather tired repertoire of jokes. I found their meaningless chit-chat comforting. "Do you think it's going to rain, love? Only I've left my washing out," or, "There was a dreadful queue at the post office." It was, as they say, very 'real'.

11

Not that I'd forgotten The Theatre. Nay, nay and thrice nay! As any actor will tell you, nothing beats poncing about in a costume or a wig and I'd had a great time over the years pretending to be a king or a servant or whatever the situation demanded.

One time, I even played a vending machine in an experimental production. Got quite good reviews for that, actually. "In turn brilliantly menacing and pitifully humble," said one. "Bunce brings unexpected passion to the role," said another.

But for me, acting was always the ultimate luxury, the most fun you could have with your clothes on. I knew I was, really, just a bit of a ham so I never, for one moment, expected to make a proper living at it, which was just as well because the roles were few and far between.

Most of the time I paid the bills with everyday jobs. I cleaned windows, I answered telephones in offices, I waited on tables and most of it was bearable enough. Eventually, when youthful enthusiasm for auditioning had waned, I took jobs behind the scenes, prop making, scenery shifting, that kind of thing.

There was one occasion, I suppose, when I did wonder just a teensy bit about what I'd missed out on. I was up for the role of Quasimodo in a musical production of 'The Hunchback of Notre Dame' called 'Hunch'. The director was beginning to make his mark in the theatre and there were rumours the production might eventually transfer to the West End.

I was thrilled to get a crack at it and I practised my stooping walk for weeks beforehand. I'm no singer but I think it's fair to say that Quasimodo himself wasn't either and I thought the audition went rather well. I would even go as far as saying it was in the bag. That was, until Toby MacInnes, or 'Tobes' as he called himself, walked in.

It was obvious straight away that Tobes was completely wrong for the role. He was too good-looking for a start, tall and blonde, like an American football player and much more leading man than misfit. I have dark, rather Mediterranean colouring, more suited to the brooding sadness of said hunchback's existence.

Nonetheless, Toby went through the audition and, call it sour grapes if you will, a very wishy-washy performance he gave.

But then, as he walked off stage, he looked at one of the interviewing panel, a woman, and winked. It was just the merest twitch of an eyelid and no doubt he was sure that no-one had seen him. But I'd seen him, alright. There was some connection between them and that wink had ensured the part would be his.

Sure enough, Toby took the role of Quasimodo. As predicted, the production was favourably reviewed although the critics were less than enthusiastic about Toby's performance. I was quite browned off about it all for a while, and I couldn't help but imagine what offers might have come my way had I played Quasimodo instead.

But I didn't let it get me down for too long. In truth, Toby didn't make it that big after all, although he pops up now and again on the telly in cameo roles as the villain's side-kick in a detective drama or as someone's long-lost brother in a soap.

But by far his biggest earner and the role that got him most exposure was that coffee advert. You know the one – young bloke, wistful, things on his mind, drives his car to the beach to watch day break. He makes himself a hot beverage in a saucepan over a camp fire and takes a big slurp just as the sun comes up. The band strikes up, he smiles and you know everything's going to be OK.

A lucky break like that was yet to be mine but at Hairs

& Graces I had found my own arena, of sorts. Quite frankly, I laid it on with a trowel. I swooped the nylon capes around the customers' shoulders, Walter Raleigh-style. I laughed loudly as they related their triumphs, I hung my head at their tales of woe. I added a few small flourishes to my behaviour such as clapping my hands to summon Suky and the trolley full of curlers to my side. I bowed low as they left.

There was only one problem. The salon only just, and I mean *only just*, made enough money to get by and after a couple of weeks, the bills started coming in. And they weren't just my bills, either. It soon became clear that the affable fellow going by the name of Mr Grant P. Worrall was a double-crossing swine who had left me with his debts.

The only way I was going to be able to pay it all off was to win the lottery and I certainly wasn't that much of a dreamer. Things looked pretty dark for a while. I just couldn't think how to turn the situation around. Then one night, I was lying on the sofa listening to a self-hypnosis tape on headphones. I was trying for the umpteenth time to give up the dreaded weed but that method didn't seem to be working any more than previous attempts.

While I listened to the rather irritating, nasal voice of the woman telling me to relax, I had half an eye on the telly. A kitsch, 1960s sci-fi movie was showing – just the kind of thing I needed to cheer me up. A team of people with silver suits and ray-guns were ambling about on the rocky terrain of some distant planet until another group of people, this time with green skin and blue, Lurex capes, leapt out from behind a boulder and captured them.

Back at alien HQ, the captives were manacled to a machine and each one had to sit under a giant, hairdryer-style thing. A green-skinned scoundrel flicked a switch, throwing his head back with a cackle, and some coloured lights flicked on and off on the dryer. After that, the silver people were released outside once again and they staggered around with glazed eyes and their arms stretched out in front like drugged-up sleepwalkers.

It was great stuff. In fact, I'd been so engrossed that I'd forgotten to pay attention to the tape. But then, a coloured light of sorts went on in my own head. An idea. One that was so utterly ridiculous that I laughed out loud. In fact, it was so ludicrous that it was worth having a bash just for the fun of it.

What if I could hypnotise my customers through the hairdryers in the salon, I wondered? What if I could persuade them to spend a bit more money? Although it was nearly eleven o'clock at night, I was so gee'd up by the idea that I hurried downstairs and started planning right away. It had worked for the alien, it could work for me. I would be that green-skinned scoundrel.

I knew a bit about electronics, again from my days in The Theatre. I found it was simple enough to fit small speakers inside the dryer hoods. I wired these up to my laptop in the office and from there, I was able to play hypnotic suggestions directly into the ears of the customers under the dryers without anyone seeing what I was up to. Even though I say so myself, it was a pretty bloody good idea.

When it came to working out exactly what I would put on the recording, I was less confident. A lot of the customers were old but they weren't your silver-surfing-pottery-classes-holiday-home-in-France kind of old. They were tartan-shopping-trolley-bingo-and-comfy-boots-from-the-small-ads old. Even if I were able to hypnotise them into parting with large wadges of cash, they wouldn't, in reality, have it to give.

I wrestled with the problem for quite a while, I can tell you. It probably sounds strange, given how things turned out, but I actually quite like old people. Some years ago, when I was a student, I took a job as a salesman. I had to telephone people, make an appointment to visit them in their homes and, once settled onto their sofas, persuade them to replace all their window frames with nasty plastic ones at great expense.

Most of the people on the list were getting on a bit. I later discovered that this was no accident. Pensioners, my boss (a horrible little oik called Nigel) informed me with a wink, were easier to wear down and more likely to sign up if you kept on at them for long enough and frightened them with tales of break-ins.

But I needed the money so I gave it a go. I put on my only suit, picked up my clipboard and knocked on doors. I travelled around courtesy of public transport so sometimes I arrived late or wet through if it was raining. My clients never seemed to mind, though. In fact, they usually took pity on me, lanky git that I was, and made a fuss of me, offering me warm towels and soup.

I was surprised to discover that the oldies didn't only talk about their operations. Some of them had lived interesting lives and enjoyed a joke. They showed me their gardens and photos of their grandchildren. They served me tea in china cups and really listened to me, more so than people my own age did, when I told them about my drama studies. Many of them actually laughed at my impersonation of Prince Charles.

The customers liked me and with most of them it would have been easy to sell them new windows twice over and a conservatory on top. But although I was desperate for the money, I could never bring myself to let anyone sign up. I always found myself talking them out of it, advising that the windows weren't really worth the money and telling them that they'd be better off spending it on their grandchildren. After three weeks and not a single sale, I was 'let go'. I still look back on that period as a happy time.

Anyhow, after several nights tossing and turning on the matter of the hypnotic dryers, I decided that the only way my conscience would allow me to pursue the scheme was if I gave something back to the old biddies of Penge rather than simply taking. It sounds rather pompous but I wanted to enrich their lives in some way. I really did.

So against a background of rolling waves, squeaking dolphins and pan pipes (taken from a couple of CDs I found at a boot fair) I recorded a disc telling these largely weatherbeaten, downtrodden women who had settled for functional hairdos and coach trips to Margate that they were the most attractive women in Penge. And you know what? They bought it. Nearly every one of those women went home smiling and feeling more confident. And, yeah, that made me feel good, too.

Of course, the recording also told them that they had to come in for weekly appointments and that they needed to buy hair care products in bulk. Well, don't forget I had rather large bills to pay. An extra tenner here and there for a box of shampoo or a few hairnets didn't seem like extortion. And when you consider that they were getting for free what you would pay a professional hypnotist fifty quid to do, I reckon they got a bargain.

So I was doing quite nicely for a while. With all the extra appointments and boxes of shampoo I was shifting, the takings were up. I'd also persuaded some of the women to bring their hubbies and friends along so I had more customers. But it was always 'just a bit off the ends'. Sometimes they wanted one of those tight, poodle numbers I call a 'bingo perm'. I could do it with my eyes shut. I started looking at the women sitting in the swivel chairs and thinking.

How would it be, I wondered, if we did something a *teensy* bit more adventurous with these women? How would their lives change if they had fashionable hair? Looked younger? Well, the idea was just too enticing to resist, wasn't it?

So I made a new recording. I still told the customers they were attractive and all that malarkey but this time, I also suggested that they would be compelled to have a radical new hairdo when they woke up. They would also, I insisted, want to pursue their innermost dreams and desires.

Blow me down, it worked! Without exception, they sat there, in front of the mirrors, and said, "Ooh, Mr Bunce. I was thinking of having something a bit different. What can you suggest?"

Sometimes they made an appointment to come back, sometimes they had it done there and then. And so they left my salon with shaven heads, extensions, curls, fringes, tufts and stripes in all the colours of the rainbow. I'm not saying these styles suited them, necessarily. In fact, many of them looked like circus freaks and I had hard time keeping a straight face. But it was *change* and God knows they needed it.

But it was the secret yearnings of their souls that really intrigued me. Sometimes the customers gave nothing away at all after a session under the dryer, bar the desire for a red Mohican or a platinum bob or whatever outlandish makeover they had in mind. But others hinted at unfulfilled ambitions or even spoke freely about new paths they intended to take.

One of our regulars, Maureen Bristow, a rather hard-bitten old bird, fell asleep under the dryer. She woke slowly, blinking and smacking her lips like a tortoise coming round from hibernation. I wasn't sure whether to offer her a cup of tea or a slice of tomato. Once fully alert, she requested a cobalt blue bob and announced with great certainty that she was going to visit 'Or-stralia' as soon as possible. We didn't see her for a few weeks after that. Had she made it Down Under or simply defected to another salon?

A young guy, camp as Christmas, and not one of our usual clients, decided it was time to go from mouse brown to blonde after his session and started singing Abba under his breath. Scandinavian leanings or just bog-standard gay man's record collection?

Another old dear asked for purple streaks and spoke wistfully of her childhood in the countryside. Whether this would result in an impulse-buy tractor or a floral housecoat was anybody's guess.

As you can see, there was a lack of closure to the process. I consoled myself with the notion that I had brought magic and excitement into these customers' lives, even if I might never find out where it led them.

Still, I had to be careful. I kept these dramatic re-styles to just two or three a week. They usually took a long time, for one thing, and I didn't want anyone to become suspicious.

As for Suky, I confided none of this to her. I was the proprietor, I reasoned, and as such I could make executive decisions without needing to consult anyone else.

I never knew quite what to say to the girl, anyway, and sometimes I got the uneasy feeling she was just humouring me. There was something otherworldly about her and she put me in mind of an elf from an old-fashioned storybook, snipping and sweeping, popping up exactly where she was needed. She never offered any information about her own life and seemed content to simply come in and get on with her work.

19

One day, during a lull in business, I was folding towels. Watery sunlight was flickering through the windows and the tumble dryer was gently humming in the background as Suky swished discarded curls into a dustpan. It was a peaceful tableau and, with nothing much on my mind, my attention was drawn once again to that peculiar substance on her head masquerading as hair.

I got to thinking.

"Ever thought of changing your style, Suky?" I asked, as casually as I could.

"Me?" she answered, barely looking up. "No, I'm happy with me 'ur as it is."

"Look, it's quiet at the moment. We haven't got another booking till four," I went on. "Why don't I give you a wash and blow-dry? On the house, of course. I've got a sample of some rather expensive new shampoo I'd like to try out."

She looked at me as if she was trying to work out what I was thinking. Then she shrugged. "OK. As long as it's quick."

We went to the wash basins at the back of the shop and she settled herself in a chair. She looked young and vulnerable sitting there, with the blue veins showing through the thin skin at her temples. As I worked the shampoo into her fuzzy little scalp, I marvelled again at the texture of her hair. It was not unlike rubbing your hand over a patch of dry grass scorched by the sun.

Afterwards, I sat her under one of the magic helmets. She protested, saying her hair was short enough to dry by itself but I insisted, telling her that the conditioner needed heat in order to work. Once the hot air was flowing, I nipped into the office and switched on the recording. Soon Suky was dozing.

Well, I could hardly contain myself while I waited. I was jigging from one foot to the other in a way that would make any Irishman proud. Not only would I be able to steer her towards a more flattering 'do', after this I would, I believed, have an insight into the inner workings of her mind.

The dryer switched off and Suky came round, moving through a range of facial expressions, from bewildered to alarmed and then, finally, ever-so-slightly disappointed when she saw me and remembered where she was.

"So!" I beamed, hands itching to get going on some new creation. "What's it to be? Extensions, perhaps? How about a leopard print pattern?"

"Eh?" she said. "What are you on about?"

"I just thought you might like a new style," I explained. "As I say, while it's quiet."

"Oh no," she said. "I told you. I'm happy with me 'ur as it is."

Surely the hypnosis had had some effect? "Any burning ambitions?" I probed. "Somewhere you've always wanted to go, anything you've always wanted to do?"

"Does Blackpool count?" she asked, wrinkling her brow with the effort.

I experienced a crushing sense of failure, not dissimilar to the sensation of flunking an audition. There was something about Suky that was immoveable, like those stubborn stains they talk about on washing powder commercials.

I was quite low for the rest of the week, actually. Even so, I kept on playing the recording to other customers with interesting results. As for Suky, she carried on as normal, seemingly unaware anything was amiss.

But, alas and alack, I was mistaken and one day things came to a head, if you'll pardon the pun.

I had sent Edna Swann, a nice old dear who used to work at the post office, home with blue stripes and

21

extensions. As soon as Edna was out of the door, Suky approached me. "Excuse me, Mr Bornce," she said, northern-style. "That lady has gone out of here looking ridiculous."

Well, I could hardly deny it, could I? She left the salon looking like a football mascot.

"Do you think so? I suppose it is a bit young for her," I replied, in what I considered a nonchalant manner.

"Young?" she gasped. "People are going to be laughing at her. Why did you let her have it done?"

I was beginning to feel a bit cornered.

"Look," I said, adopting a firm tone. "It's nothing to do with me if someone comes in here wanting something a bit unusual. I simply do as I'm asked." Then I added, just to remind her who was running the show, "Now get back on with your work."

Suky left the room. A few moments later she came back and stood in front of me holding a CD.

"What?" I shrugged.

"You tell me," she demanded.

"It's a CD," I stalled.

"Brainwash, set and blow-dry, perhaps?" she quizzed.

I'd been rumbled good and proper.

Improvisation is part of the actor's tool kit but my mind was buzzing with so many thoughts, I didn't know what to do or say next. Should I break down sobbing? Tell her I was mentally ill? Bribe her to keep quiet? Where would I get the money, anyway? I wasn't sure whether, technically speaking, I had even broken the law.

In the end I went for the 'pity' option. "I just wanted to help," I whined. I attempted a pleading look round the eyes.

"Help," she echoed. "How do blue stripes help an eighty-year-old woman? Or rainbow stripes? Or plaits?"

"I wanted to shake them all up a bit. Make a change," I

went on. "You know what they say, new hairstyle, new life. And I needed the dosh and all that…" I faltered.

Suky turned and walked slowly towards the door, looking downwards, apparently deep in thought. She picked up a hairbrush and examined it, and then swivelled on her heel to face me. Her ability to create dramatic tension was spot on, I had to admit.

"I've wanted to be an 'ur dresser all me life. I came doan 'ere—"

"Where?" I queried. "Oh. Sorry. You meant 'down here'. Carry on," I blustered, anxious to avoid antagonising her any more. Northerners hate it when people pick them up on their accents, especially posh gits like me.

"Mr Worrall knew me auntie. I came doan from Bolton to work for him," she continued. She pointed to the fuzz on top of her head. "See with this, I could never do the things other girls did with clips and bows and the like, so I wanted to do it to other people's 'ur." She paused and stared into the distance, her feline eyes moistening. "I know what it's like to have a dream."

Well, I could see where she was coming from, alright, but not necessarily where she was going. "So, er, you're not going to call the police, or anything like that?" I said.

"I want to be creative director," she announced. "I want to do this place up and I want you" – she jabbed the hairbrush at me – "to include me in all decisions."

"Fine! Great!" I enthused. "But we can still do the hypnosis thing, right? It's just that the money, you know. Kind of handy…"

Suky nodded slowly like a queen granting special dispensation to one of her courtiers. "So long as I have a say."

I'd clearly underestimated her. She would have made a cracking Lady Macbeth.

I was somewhat uneasy when I went down to the salon the next morning. It was true, Suky had appeared satisfied with the outcome of our discussion and had made no mention of calling in the authorities. But who was to say she hadn't thought better of it overnight? How could I be sure the boys in blue wouldn't be waiting to escort me to the local cop shop?

But she turned up as usual, not a truncheon in sight, carrying a large tin of paint and a couple of sponge rollers.

"Poor-ple," she said.

That afternoon, after the last customer had departed, under Suky's direction I rolled up my sleeves and painted two of the walls a kind of aubergine colour. Classy, I admit, though the colour did seem to absorb a lot of light.

"Makes it more cosy," she assured me. I wasn't going to argue.

Then we threw the nets, posters and wrought iron furniture in a nearby skip and rollered the other walls brilliant white. Suky had got hold of a few mirrors that were edged in silver mosaic tiles and looked rather modish. She had also bought a pile of matching, purple towels from the market. It was so simple to transform the place, I wondered why I hadn't thought of it before.

Then she turned her attention to yours truly.

"This'll have to go," she said, pointing at my favourite, cream-coloured, belted cardigan. True, it was a bit 'seventies, but I rather liked it. "You need a black shirt."

I couldn't help thinking that she was the one who ought to be wearing a black shirt, though for different reasons.

"Your 'ur needs a tidy-up, too," she went on and she took me by the shoulders and steered me towards a chair.

I sat down and faced forward while she pulled at sections of my unruly mane, cocking her head to one side as she considered what to do. The grey was really creeping in these days, I noticed, and my sideburns could do with a trim. My eyes, which a director had once described as 'dark and brooding' now looked a little hangdog.

"Now, see here," I cautioned. "I don't want—" But it was too late. She whipped a tiny pair of scissors from her overall pocket and set about me, flickety-flicking, until at least three inches of my crowning glory lay scattered on the lino. But I had to admit, the girl done good. I looked much better.

From that day onwards, things were different at Hairs & Graces. Suky was still, technically speaking, my employee though she behaved more like an equal, sometimes even telling me what to do. She even started doing the double-handclap to summon me to her side. Annoyingly, I found myself following her instructions.

It wasn't such a bad thing. She was pretty good at what she did and had a good sense of what colours and styles suited people. The customers were happy. Money was coming in and one day we might be in credit.

But things were different inside me, too, and not necessarily for the better. I drifted around the salon in my black shirt, fiddling with bottles and hairdryers, half-heartedly tidying things away. I spent more time than I should outside on ciggie-breaks. In short, I didn't have the heart for it any more.

Lying on my second-hand sofa in the evenings, I wondered why, now that I had a tantalising glimpse of success, I felt so dismal. And then it came to me – I was living someone else's dream.

Young Suky had clearly dreamt of becoming a hairdresser with her own salon for much of her life and now she had that, courtesy of Rafe Bunce and his Amazing Hypnotic Dryers. While I'd had a laugh working in the salon, it had never really been more than a jolly wheeze, just another theatrical production. Now it had become all business-like.

Salvation arrived the very next morning in the form of me old mucker Dave. I've always found life's 'Daves' to be refreshingly normal and he was no exception. He texted me to say he was taking a fringe production to the Edinburgh Festival. His Prince Charles had dropped out unexpectedly – would I step into the breach? Not much money in it, he warned, but he was paying expenses and it promised to be a good gig.

Well, I didn't need to think twice, did I? Suky didn't need me, she could manage very well on her own. She would keep things ticking over, pay herself a wage. Maybe one day I could even sell her the place? But for now, my own personal sat-nav was sending me in a new direction. After all, as The Bard so aptly puts it, "All the world's a stage."

I slung my gear in the back of my camper van and set off. I would have to say that that van had been my most faithful female companion over the years, sad individual that I am. Don't ask me why cars are always women. I don't make the rules.

We'd had some good times together, me and that van. In the 'seventies, I painted it purple and drove round Europe in it. Later, when I was working in The Theatre and travelling round the country, I kipped in it on many occasions when I couldn't get lodgings. It's pretty clapped-out now but it would probably cost more than it's worth to fix it up. Still, I can't bring myself to get shot of it. Too many memories.

But on the way to meet Dave, there was something I wanted to do. I'd been thinking about Tobes and that advert and I was seized with the urge to go to the coast and watch the sun rise. Tacky, yes, idiotic, quite probably, but I needed some kind of dramatic gesture to get back into my groove.

I got as far as Croydon. The blasted van, whose engine had been making noises like a cappuccino machine, finally spluttered to a halt just past the airport. I pulled over to the side of the road and looked under the bonnet, just for the sake of it, really, as I didn't have a clue what I was looking for.

There was nothing to do but sit and wait for the breakdown people to come. And so I was not relaxed by sea breezes ruffling my hair nor comforted by the timeless swish of waves rolling onto a deserted beach. No, I wasn't to be allowed to wallow in such romantic fantasies that particular morning. Instead, I watched the sun come up over the back of a retail park on the A23, breathing in the fumes of passing juggernauts. Story of my bloody life.

Roots

Hetty first saw the tree the day her divorce came through. She'd been on the bus on her way back from Croydon when she spotted it growing in the middle of a roundabout.

It was in full bloom, with juicy, pale purple blossoms like cupped hands, and it stood there politely ignoring the office blocks and trams that surrounded it.

Like me, Hetty thought. Stuck in the wrong place. After that she always inwardly greeted the tree whenever she went past.

Of course, she and plants had what the man in the flat next door called 'previous', although she knew he was talking about something other than gardening.

Growing up on the family farm in Norfolk, she'd wandered the fields and woodland for hours and knew all the names of the wild flowers, like sneezewort, ragged robin, lady's mantle and corn cockle. She knew the birds, too, and could do a passable impersonation of some of them. Better than her brothers, even.

But she was sixteen before she set eyes on a magnolia tree. She'd gone to her first proper dance at a neighbouring farm. The family were quite well-off and there were people playing stringed instruments and cocktails which had burned her throat and made her head spin.

Several young men asked her to dance and when she stepped out onto the terrace to get some air, there, perfectly colour-co-ordinated under the lilac sky, was the most beautiful tree she'd ever seen with big, creamy blossoms that looked like they were made of sugar paste. That moment felt to Hetty like an unfurling.

That had all been 'BC' though. Before Concrete, Before Clive, her husband, had uprooted her and moved her to a more man-made part of the country. Fifty years on and she

28

still thought of it as temporary, though she'd done her best with the garden. She'd planted lavender, delphiniums and an apricot-coloured rose called, Queen Mab, and people were often surprised at how it looked more like a cottage garden than a back yard outside a council block.

These days, in fact, ever since she'd had her hair done, Hetty often woke up feeling agitated, like there was something she'd forgotten to do. It was that time of year, all beginnings and endings, babies and break-ups, and the lightening mornings and new shoots always gave her a surge of nervous energy.

One Monday, as she pottered about in her yard, watering and tidying, she got to thinking about the tree again and how it was alone on that roundabout, unappreciated and unloved, apart from the odd visit from council workers who would pick up the dead leaves and mow the surrounding grass.

When there was a problem, you sorted it. That was the way she'd been brought up and Hetty decided, then, what she would do.

Her friend Barbara, who lived nearby, had a son who was a builder and owned a truck with an open back. She looked surprised when Hetty asked if she could borrow it but agreed. It was true, Hetty didn't actually have a licence, but that was no matter – she had driven the farm vehicles often enough in her youth to know what she was doing but Barbara didn't need to know that.

She set off after midnight and found that driving the truck proved as easy as she remembered. The roads were quiet and in twenty minutes she was there. The air was still and mild as milk against her skin and a section of moon shone out from behind a cloud to help her with her task. It had been a dry spring and the ground was tough and it took all the strength of her four foot eleven frame to force the spade into the soil but she couldn't rush. If she damaged the roots, it might not survive.

Once the soil was loosened around the base, she pulled at the trunk, trying to drag the tree from the hole and onto a sheet of polythene so she could wrap it up. "Come on my old friend!" she whispered. "Let's be having you," but it wouldn't budge. Exhausted, she sank back onto her heels, covered her face and wept like she hadn't done in years.

When she looked up again, she discovered she wasn't alone on the roundabout. Two teenage boys, clutching cans of cider and wearing baggy jeans that dragged on the ground and hooded sweatshirts that hung from sloping shoulders, were looming over her.

"You alright, love?" one of them asked. "Only, we heard you crying."

"We're on our way home," the other boy added.

Hetty was so relieved to hear a kindly voice that she started crying all over again. "It's just too heavy for me," she sighed.

"We'll give you a hand if you like," the first one shrugged, as if seeing an old woman digging up a tree in the dead of night was an everyday situation.

"Yeah! Why not?" the other boy nodded.

They put down their cans, taking great care not to spill the contents, and lunged at the tree, scuffing at the roots to loosen them further.

"This should do it!" one called, giving her the thumbs up sign.

Seeing them rough up her beloved tree in this way, Hetty wailed and begged them to be careful but as she spoke the magnolia sprang loose in a rustle of leaves, sending one of the youths staggering across the roundabout. She had to hide her eyes as they parcelled the roots up in the plastic sheet and loaded it into the back of the truck.

Having earned their 'consoling elderly women' badge, the would-be scouts waved her off, giving her the thumbs up again. By the time she got back to Penge, she was shaking with exhaustion but exhilarated, too, like she'd been doused with cold water.

Her arms and legs ached so much the following day she could hardly get out of bed but she shuffled downstairs and put the kettle on. Outside the kitchen window she could see the captive, still wrapped in plastic and looking a little droopy. "Won't be long," she trilled. "I'll be out to see you shortly."

On the telly a young woman with marigold skin and a buttercup-coloured jacket was chirping out the local news but Hetty was hardly paying attention. There was a clod of trodden-in dirt on the carpet and she worried at it with her fingernail.

But then something else caught her eye.

Some black and white CCTV footage came on and although the movements were jerky, you could just about make out three figures dragging something across a roundabout. The chirpy woman's voice was deeper now, and more serious, speaking in the tones a headmistress might use, warning members of the public not to approach the suspects in case they were dangerous.

Hetty started shaking so much that her cup was clattering on the saucer. She'd never had so much as a library fine and now it hit her that she really had broken the law. How could that be when she was only trying to help? Those poor boys! They wouldn't hurt a fly! Who would employ them now with criminal records? She imagined how angry her father would be, even though he'd been dead for more than twenty years. This had all gone very wrong indeed.

Still shaking, she decided that there was only one thing to do. She dashed upstairs and put on the first clothes she could find, a plum-coloured fleece and turquoise jogging bottoms, coming down and almost falling over the mud-caked wellies as she shoved her feet into them once more. Outside, she dragged the tree through the side gate and into the street.

The man from next door was ambling past and he stopped, casting a sly eye over Hetty's activities.

"That a tree you got there?" he asked.

"It is," she nodded. "Would you be so kind as to put it in the truck for me? I'm in a dreadful hurry."

"No worries," the man shrugged, doing as she asked. "You taking it somewhere? Is it a gift or somefink?"

"That's right," she agreed, speaking firmly to control the tremor in her voice. "A gift."

Hetty clambered into the driver's seat and closed the door, feeling sure that her neighbour would be straight onto the police as soon as she'd gone. She was trembling so much she could hardly get the key into the ignition but then the truck spluttered into life and she roared away from the kerb, just missing a man on a bike. She headed north across the river, banging her hands on the steering wheel every time she encountered a red light, desperate to escape.

Eventually, though, she made it across the city and out, at last, onto an open stretch of motorway. She rolled down the window and let the breeze batter against her skin as she picked up speed, swerving from lane to lane, going as fast as the old truck would allow. She found herself singing 'Old Brown's Daughter', a song from her youth that she thought she'd forgotten.

But after nearly four hours on the road, Hetty began to feel light-headed. No surprise as she'd had nothing to eat since the night before and only a few sips of tea that morning. Spotting a sign for a service station, she swerved onto the exit ramp just in time, pushing hard on the brake.

She couldn't remember the last time she'd been to such a place. Everywhere there was movement, like looking down a microscope at a swarming colony of bacteria. Vehicles pulled in and out of spaces among rows and rows of parked cars. Hot, tired families walked about squinting at plastic signs. Lights flashed on and off.

Hetty parked in the first space she came to. The police couldn't be far behind, she was sure, so she went into a fast food outlet and wolfed down a burger in just a few mouthfuls, giving herself hiccups and raising the eyebrows of the family sitting next to her.

Minutes later she was back behind the wheel, joining a queue of cars heading for the exit. But although she had refuelled herself, she had neglected to check the truck's petrol gauge and the engine started to judder.

"Blast!" she muttered but managed to steer it up the kerb and onto a grass verge before it groaned to a complete halt.

Hetty slumped forward onto the steering wheel, too tired even to cry. "Now what?" she wondered aloud. When she lifted her head again, she looked in the rear-view mirror and saw an elderly woman, whom she hardly recognised, with Perspex glasses and wild, white, wind-blown hair streaked purple, looking back at her with frightened eyes the colour of forget-me-nots.

And then she caught the reflection of the magnolia in the back. All the flowers and most of the leaves had gone, blown away down the motorway, she imagined, like a trail of confetti. The tree was now sad and bare.

A breakdown recovery man, who had been standing by a display hoping to recruit new members, went over when he heard the sobbing but Hetty took one look at his uniform and started screaming.

By the time the police came, she was sitting in the back of the truck, arms wrapped round the trunk, whispering, "What have I done?" over and over again. She was only a couple of miles from the village where she'd grown up.

Sanctuary

Darren squinted into the mirror and wiped at the spattered toothpaste with the sleeve of his dressing gown.

"Jesus, Mary and Joseph!" he muttered. "What was I thinking?"

It hadn't looked so bad a couple of days ago. The bulb had gone again in the living room and in the gloom, after a couple of tequilas, he'd convinced himself that it was almost silvery – sort of 'thirties starlet crossed with that woman off the telly with the shoulder pads. Now, under the strip lighting, he had to admit it looked like someone had chucked a bucket of custard over his head.

Still, that was what you got, he supposed, for going to a grannies' hairdresser. Not that place where Nana Pat used to go, mind. Up there, mullets and moustaches were still paraded around as the height of sophistication, and that was just the women.

No, this had been Linda's idea. She'd heard him sniffing in the next booth, peered over and seen him all blotchy, and put two and two together.

Her grandma, she told him, lived on a barge and wore ethnic print trousers. She was a free spirit, even had dreadlocks, which she had done at a salon not far from where he lived. Dirt cheap, it was. Changed her life. Why didn't he get down there for a makeover?

"Do you a world of good, Daz," she said. "Show Enrico what you're made of."

Now, with his new, canary-coloured thatch making his complexion look even pinker, what he was made of looked to be sodding Plasticine. Or Spam. Either way Enrico would probably never speak to him again.

He felt a cold needle of irritation for Linda's right-on gran, even though he'd never met her. Why couldn't she just stay at home smelling of wee and knitting cardigans like other old people? Why did she have to go round inspiring people?

Darren splashed his face with water and was about to give his hands a quick blast under the drier when he remembered he had to be dead careful. Wiping them instead on his bath robe, he slowly opened the door a crack and peeped out.

All was quiet and dark with just a lamp here and there giving off enough soft light to show the way. He edged out through the gap, letting the door close little-by-little so that it wouldn't bang, and followed the arrows on the floor to the bedroom area.

Last night he'd tried 'Funkig', a teenage-style room with built-in storage and a desk unit. Right comfy, it was, though he was sure the zany duvet cover would be vomit-inducing for any teenager who'd had a session on the pop.

Tonight he'd decided he would stay in 'Världsvan' across the way. It was all chrome and moody black and white photos and reminded him of what he'd imagined living in London might be like before he actually got there and discovered the stone-clad-patterned-carpet-nightmare of Wendover Road.

At 'Bend Over Road', as Enrico liked to call it, just walking into the kitchen could give you food poisoning. The plates had that much filth on them, they looked like petri dishes and all the mugs were stained brown like tramps' teeth.

He'd told them all loads of times. Said that if he had to scour the sink one more time, he was going to flip his lid. But Jackie, the one who looked like a bus driver in drag, had just laughed and told him to 'chill out'.

Well, that was exactly what he was doing now so she could take her charcoaled saucepan and shove it.

Maybe all that bleach had gone to his brain but he'd developed a craving for clean lines and fresh cotton. He yearned for fjords and pine forests. He wanted clean people with sing-song voices and a place where a person with yellow hair could pass unnoticed. He'd come down here on the tram. Not Stockholm, exactly, but it would do for now.

He put his headphones on and pressed 'play'. When the bouzouki started, he recognised it as one of his favourites, joining in with Agnetha and Anni-Frid's tinsel-like harmonies as he wandered between the displays, yearning for angels and for dreams to come true.

A basket of plastic washing-up brushes shaped like flowers announced themselves as 'Tulpan – only 50p each'. Dead clever, these Scandies. Made you want to buy things you never knew you needed. He helped himself to one, using it as a makeshift microphone as the song reached a crescendo, screwing his eyes shut tight and clenching his fist towards his chest like he'd seen them do on talent shows.

Finally, the music finished and he took a deep breath of woody air, completing the performance by lowering his arms and exhaling slowly. He opened his eyes, cleansed. He felt free.

Twenty feet away, the outline blurred by the darkness, a figure sat in one of the plywood chairs, watching.

Darren jolted like he had been wired up to jump leads. "Christ on a bike!" he screamed, staggering backwards into a basket of turquoise, plastic toast racks labelled 'Knaprig' and sprawling on the floor.

The figure stood up and came slowly towards him.

Darren snatched the headphones from his ears and heaved himself to his feet. "Who the bloody 'ell are you? What are you doing?" he shrieked.

The mysterious onlooker was a man. "Steady on, son,

steady on," he cautioned, raising his hands. "I don't mean you no harm."

He looked to be in his seventies and spoke in the reassuring tones you might expect from a gardener advising someone on protecting their dahlias from frost. He was wearing beige trousers, padded shoes and a beige, zip-up jacket. His grey eyes looked careworn. No uniform, then, but still.

"Look, I haven't taken anything," Darren pleaded, desperate to get away. "I'll just get my things and—"

"Alan," the man smiled, holding out his hand. "And you are?"

Darren couldn't think of a reason to refuse so he shook the man's hand, peering past him for the Way Out sign and wondering whether he could make a dash for it without setting off an alarm. "Er... my friends call me Daz. Is there...?"

"Why don't you come and have a sit-down, Daz?" Alan continued like they were old friends, putting a hand on Darren's shoulder blade and steering him round the corner towards the living room section. "We've got a brew on."

We, he'd said. Did that mean there was a whole bunch of security guards lurking behind a shelving unit, waiting to throw him to the floor and frisk him? He'd seen it happen once in a bookshop and the bloke hadn't even stolen anything. But then they came to a three-piece suite covered in striped canvas and Alan stopped.

"This here is Daz," he announced to a young man with a goatee who was lying on the sofa, feet up, reading a magazine. "Daz, I'd like you to meet MC Sparkplug."

If this guy was a security guard, he certainly didn't take his job too seriously. He was wearing a scruffy, green T-shirt, jeans and trainers and simply nodded and raised one finger by way of a greeting and carried on reading.

37

"Been here since last week," Alan whispered. "Girlfriend kicked him out. Not in a good 'headspace', as you young people say. Take a seat," he went on. "Builders' do you?"

He picked up a shiny, red thermos from a nearby coffee table and poured brown liquid into a mug which he handed to Darren.

"Got some of those cinnamon biscuits that they sell downstairs," Alan said, offering him a packet. "Lovely with a cuppa."

"Came here with the wife, I did," he went on, perching on the end of the sofa. "Saturday, was it? Or maybe Sunday. I forget. Anyway, she goes off to look at kitchens and I settle down, nice comfy armchair and the paper. Before I know it, I've dozed off," he chuckled. "Easily done when you get to my age."

He took a mouthful of tea and swallowed loudly. "When I wake up, I'm confused about where I am. I follow the arrows on the floor through the lighting department, past the kids' section, and so forth, but every time I try to get out, I find myself back in the same place. So I go to the toilet and when I come out, all the lights are off and everyone's gone home. That's when I met Sparkplug, here."

"Showed him the ropes," Sparkplug agreed from behind his magazine.

Darren sank into his armchair. He couldn't work out what he'd got himself into at the Mad Hatter's hotel but he was going to be pigging well stuck there till morning. He half wished someone would come and arrest him.

It was always the same. At the call centre, when he phoned people to ask if they had ever been involved in an accident that wasn't their fault, people usually said yes they had and told him all about it, in vivid detail, too.

"Didn't your wife wonder where you'd gone?" he asked.

"Ah, that's where one of these comes in," Alan smiled, taking a mobile phone from his coat pocket. "My grandson got it for me last Christmas. The missus had already gone home, of course, when she couldn't find me. So I call her and say I'm going away for a few days. We've got a caravan in Canvey, like. Said Big Dave from the pub was giving me a lift up there."

"She didn't mind?" Darren asked. He couldn't imagine Nana Pat letting his granddad disappear for days with no explanation.

Alan waved his hand as if the details were unimportant. "Nah, she was just glad to have me out from under her feet, wasn't she?" he carried on. "Always fussing, she is. Hoovering round me. Soon as you've finished your drink, she whisks the cup away. It's exhausting. That's why I thought I might as well hang about here for a while. Beautiful, isn't it?"

He pronounced it 'bewdiful' and waved his hand around, beaming, as if he were living it up in a stately home.

There was a sudden 'slap' as MC Sparkplug tossed his magazine onto the floor. He sat up and swung round to face Darren, staring right at him. His dark brown eyes seemed to absorb all light, what little there was of it in there.

"See, you've got to get your head round the system," he advised, tapping his forehead. "There's always a system wherever you go. I'm a night owl but Alan here is up with the dawn chorus. I keep an eye on things in the small hours and he's up early, making the tea. We're like the yin and yang, me and Alan. Washing in the toilets, however, tricky situation," he nodded. "So we've both got our slots. Makes things easier."

Alan agreed that this was perfectly true.

"I saw you last night over there," Sparkplug went on, nodding towards the teenage-style room. "I don't want to make a big deal of it but strictly speaking, that's my bed."

"Yours?" Darren almost choked with surprise. What was this? The Three sodding Bears? What gave him the right to tell him what he could and couldn't do?

"I was here before you, mate," Sparkplug pushed.

"Well you needn't worry yourself," Darren snapped. "I'll be in that black and white room tonight. Sleep where you like."

Sparkplug and Alan exchanged glances. "Well... the thing is," Alan went on. "It's Big Dave..."

"Big Dave?"

"He's sort of got his eye on that one and I'd hate to disappoint him," Alan shrugged, "what with his back and all that. He'll be along later. He's just having a bit of 'me time' over in soft furnishings."

"We're just saying, that's all," Sparkplug flopped back onto the sofa, snapping a biscuit in half. "Chill out, dude."

Jaw clenching, Darren stood up. "Well, gentlemen, this is all very nice," he sighed, "but nature calls. Just going to powder my nose. Back in a mo."

He went back the way he had come, hurrying as fast as he could without actually breaking into a run. Before he reached the toilets, he skittered left into an area where there were different types of storage on display. When he came to a wardrobe, part of the 'Enkelhet' beech veneer, budget range, he slipped inside and closed the door.

It was cramped and smelt of sawdust but, if he turned his knees sideways, there was just room for him to perch his buttocks on a shelf. He stayed there, still, like a fox in its lair, barely daring to breathe.

It wasn't what you'd call luxurious but it was the only place he was going to get any solitude. In the morning he

40

would sneak out and retrieve his things and get the hell out of there and back to Wendover Road.

After a few minutes he heard footsteps and murmuring voices.

"Where'd he go?" Alan was wondering aloud. "Probably got lost. He'll turn up in Lighting tomorrow, I shouldn't wonder."

Sparkplug spoke. "Do you think he was…?"

"What, Swedish?" Alan chuckled. "Course he was. You saw his hair, didn't you?"

Dreadful Man

Sylvia was waiting for the bus. The shelter, like all the others in Penge, was scrawled with mysterious, teenage hieroglyphics and the surrounding pavement pock-marked with chewing gum. Diseased-looking, it was.

She clasped her shopping bag a little closer. A neighbour had told her that cod was on special in Marks and she hoped she'd be able to get her hands on some before it ran out. Brian would be expecting it for his tea.

A tatty red van pulled up across the road and a man leant out. His skin was the colour of lacquered wood and his hair was twisted into what young people called 'dreadlocks', with a sprinkling of grey like someone had dusted him with icing sugar.

He called out, "Hey, Sister!"

Sylvia looked round to see who he was talking to but found she was the only person there.

"Yeah, you, Sister," he repeated. "Come over here. Come, come."

Brian had always told her to steer clear of 'foreign types'. Most of them, he said, were over here taking advantage of free hospitals and schools. He knew people who had been to Spain, he said, and they had told him all about what your Continental waiter could get up to.

Sylvia had always thought that Spain looked rather nice, though she didn't say so.

So, normally, she would have ignored the man in the van. Walked off, looked the other way. But that day, for some reason, she went over.

"Can I help you?" she asked, but the man started laughing with a kind of 'yuk-yuk' sound, gold tooth winking as it caught the light.

"I was looking for the way to the Croydon Road," he

answered in a voice that sounded as rich and brown as his skin. "But now I see you an' you look like an interesting woman," he went on, glancing at her hair. "How about I give you a lift somewhere?"

Sylvia sighed. Here we go again, she thought. Since she'd got her own dreadlocks done at the salon last week, she'd been getting a lot of peculiar attention. People had stared. The woman from the laundrette certainly had a good old gawp. Even dropped the packet of soap powder she was carrying.

As for Brian, all the colour had drained from his face when he saw her and he'd spent the rest of the day in his shed. When he came out, he told her he was disappointed and that her hair looked like bits of mangled Brillo pad. The next day her cousin, Wanda, had offered to give the hairdo a saucer of milk.

But Sylvia wasn't bothered. Let them say what they liked. She'd long ago given up on compliments.

Still, no-one had ever said '*wo-maaan*' to her quite like that before. All deep and rumbly, like something about to erupt. So she got in the passenger seat. Climbed into that red van as if it was the kind of thing she did every day.

Inside had a funny, sweet smell a bit like toilet freshener. A little green, yellow and black flag saying 'Jamaica' was dangling from the rear-view mirror and reggae music was playing softly in the background. Brian usually listened to organ concertos when they were in the car.

"The name's Garston," the man said, leaning across and taking her hand. His long knotty fingers were smooth and dry like driftwood. "And you are, Sister?"

"Sylvia," she squeaked quickly, in case she had one of her blank moments. She didn't want him to think she was daft, did she?

"Sylvia," he drawled, smiling. The way he said it made her think of warm beaches and suntan lotion instead of the dusty, ballroom frocks and lipstick-smeared teeth it normally brought to mind.

"So, Sylvia," he went on, "how about we go someplace for a cup o' coffee?"

"Well, I was on my way to the shops..." she hesitated. "Is there time?"

"Always time for the good things in life," Garston replied and he chuckled in that yuk-yuk way again.

He restarted the engine and pulled off into the traffic, hardly noticing the car behind him hooting furiously as he swerved into the middle of the road. He turned up the radio and started singing along, tapping his fingers on the steering wheel, even closing his eyes at certain points in the song, which made Sylvia somewhat uneasy, though mostly she was content to be in the warm, watching colours and shapes of the outside world drifting past. Neither of them spoke much.

Finally Garston pulled up outside a café bearing a sign, hand-painted in earthy shades, saying 'Karibbean Kitchen'. It wasn't far from where she lived but she'd never noticed it before.

"Come, Sister. Let's go have something to drink," he announced, walking ahead. He was wearing white overalls daubed with paint and, Sylvia noticed, he wasn't as tall as he'd looked sitting down.

She followed him inside. The place was sparsely decorated and empty, apart from a young man with dreadlocks of his own and a bright, yellow T-shirt with 'Groovy' printed in orange lettering. He was leaning on the counter reading a newspaper.

Garston called out to him and punched the air by way of a greeting, the bunch of keys at his waist jingling. He led her to a table near the window and their chairs honked loudly on the wooden floorboards as they sat down.

Sylvia's glasses misted up in the warm and she wiped them on the sleeve of her raincoat. "This is nice," she ventured, noticing the lime green and orange tablecloth and the little vase of red plastic flowers. She wasn't sure they really were 'nice' but you had to say something, didn't you?

But she hadn't even picked up the menu when the man in the yellow shirt came over, putting coffee and bricks of sticky cake that looked like cavity wall insulation down in front of them. They smelt of spice and black treacle.

Garston slapped him on the back and murmured something Sylvia couldn't understand. Then he started humming once more and tapping the table as if she wasn't even there, swaying to a melody only he could hear.

Sylvia felt then like she'd stumbled into some kind of Rastafarian tea party where she couldn't work out the rules. Well, she had better things to do, thank you very much. Might as well put a stop to this nonsense and get back to her shopping. She pushed her chair back and was about to set off in search of another bus stop when Garston suddenly halted his routine and looked at her, beady-eyed as a cockerel.

"You got a husband, Sylvia?" he said.

"I have," she confirmed. She cleared her throat. "His name is Brian."

"Well, he sure is one lucky man," Garston sniggered, seizing her hand in his dry palm once again. She wasn't sure what the joke was but she tried to smile.

He then decided to share a few of his philosophies about life. Sylvia had no choice but to sit back down and take a mouthful of cake, which, she found, wasn't too bad.

"Nice and moist, innit?" he winked.

"Music is very important to me," Garston went on,

45

stirring his coffee. "Got to have it on day and night, at home, in the van, wherever. What about you, Sylvia?"

It had been years since anyone had quizzed her on her musical tastes. "Well, I quite like Cliff Richard," she ventured but as soon as she said it, she wished she'd kept quiet.

But Garston didn't mock. "Mmm-hmm," he nodded, considering her words. "He is a God-fearin' man, that's for sure."

Sylvia asked him what he liked to listen to but he didn't seem to hear. Instead, he offered that he loved a cold beer on a hot day and that he believed too many people in the world expected something for nothing. He was a man, he said, who liked to be straight with people. He always told the truth. His son Lester was hoping to be a musician himself some day.

Sylvia asked Garston if he had any other children.

People weren't respecting Mother Earth, he went on, tapping his fork on the plate to emphasise the point. Look at the floods and fires, look at the famine, he said.

With that voice, all warm and relaxing like a hot bath, Sylvia would have been happy to hear him read out the ingredients on a tin of soup. But, she realised with dismay, give or take a hairdo and a syrupy delivery, she might as well be at home listening to her husband banging on. The world, it seemed, was full of Brians.

Garston knocked back the last mouthful of his coffee and clattered the cup back on the saucer. "Come, Sister. I'll take you home," he announced.

But that nice, posh man at the hairdresser had asked her about her dreams and Sylvia hadn't forgotten that. "No," she replied, the gold hoops in her earlobes flickering like the leaves on a poplar as she moved. "I'm not ready to leave yet."

Garston's eyebrows sprang several inches up his forehead and his eyes stretched wide. "Not ready, you say?"

"No," she repeated. "I want to dance."

"You want to dance..."

"Well, yes," Sylvia went on, shifting in her seat. She knew that she sounded foolish but she couldn't go back now. "I want to learn to dance to that 'reggy' music."

At first she wasn't sure whether Garston was having some kind of seizure. He leant forward, wheezing heavily. She'd done that first aid course at work, it was true, but that had been years ago and she wasn't sure she could remember how to help him. But when he sat up again, wiping his eyes, she saw that he was laughing.

"Troy! Troy!" he bellowed to the waiter. Sylvia thought for a moment that he was yelling 'try!' and wondered what the boy was supposed to be attempting, but then she realised it was just Garston's accent.

"Get some music on, boy! Get some Bob Marley going," he went on.

After a bit of clunking and crackling, the soft twang of a bass guitar, drums and Bob Marley's distinctive voice came through a loudspeaker and filled the room. Garston took the cup from Sylvia's hand and put it down, pulling her to her feet. He led her to a space in the middle of the floor.

"You see, you got to *feel* the music," he explained, closing his eyes and swaying from side to side, hands in his pockets. He joined in, singing softly.

Sylvia, still unsure of the rules, copied his movements. She was wearing some of those ballet pumps that her daughter had bought her from the market. They were easy to move around in but she was conscious that her bunions were sticking out like a pair of elbows.

"Ah! You're gettin' it now," Garston prompted, sneaking a sideways glance.

Troy appeared on the other side of Sylvia. "That's right," he coaxed. "Now raise your 'ands like this, nice and easy." He lifted his arms up and down one at a time like a puppet pulled by strings. His voice was lighter and younger than Garston's.

"Now bend the knees a little further," Garston joined in. "Like you going to sit down but you change your mind."

Sylvia did as they suggested. It wasn't so hard after all, she found. No different to what she'd done in her kitchen many times listening to the radio.

The three of them danced together, each in their separate worlds, for a few more minutes through another track. Sylvia closed her eyes, too, at peace, swaying to the music as if the Karibbean Kitchen on a Monday afternoon was exactly where she was meant to be.

Then the door whined open. "Cup of tea to go, mate?" said a man in a hard hat and fluorescent coat, and the spell was broken.

They went back to the red van. As they drove back to Penge, Garston told Sylvia of his beliefs on schools and bringing up children and why he was absolutely certain that Elvis was still alive. She 'Oh-ed' and 'Ah-ed' in the right places but wasn't really listening.

He insisted on dropping her back right outside her front door and she clambered out, feeling like those people in the films who find themselves dumped at the side of the road, bewildered and squinting at the sunlight.

"See you again, Sylvia. I'll call round next time I is passin'," he smiled, his gold tooth glinting again. "It's been nice meetin' you, Sister." He pressed the hooter twice as he drove off.

"Not if I see you first," she muttered under her breath.

"Where on Earth have you been?" Brian asked, coming to the front door as she let herself in. "It's gone four o'clock!"

"Oh, nowhere much," she sighed. Well, there was nothing to say, was there? Her outing hadn't amounted to much more than the froth on her coffee.

"Did you get the shopping?" he went on.

"Actually, we're having something different," Sylvia told him.

"Different?" Brian gasped. "Not curry! You know how I feel about curry—"

Yes, she knew how he felt about curry. She knew his opinions on most things. "I'm making jerk chicken tonight," she announced. "Like they have in Jamaica."

It was the second time in a matter of days that her husband had been struck dumb. Sylvia thought she could get to like it.

Mr Denny's Leg

"His *leg*?" Sheila swallowed her mouthful of wine a bit too quickly and her voice came out rough as a smoker's rasp.

"He was always putting it up on the desk, wasn't he?" Val went on. "He'd be giving it all the 'je m'appelle' and what-have-you, and... wallop! Up it went. Right, bang, slap. Next to Jackie, usually."

She remembered it so clearly. The sun-starved limb emerging from brown, polyester trousers gone shiny from too much wear. The colourless hairs poking out at all angles like crushed crane flies. The beige sock. The padded lace-up. "I just keep thinking about it, that's all."

She took a deep breath and looked up at the ceiling. It wouldn't do to get all tearful, tonight of all nights. It was sad, and all that, but she didn't want anyone thinking she was soft. You couldn't cry over someone's leg, could you? It wouldn't make sense.

"Jackie Beveridge?" Sheila quizzed. "The one who supported West Ham and wore all that eyeliner? Is she coming?"

"Should've seen her face," Val added. "She used to look at it like someone had put a bowl of sick in front of her."

Sheila clunked her wine glass down, almost tipping it over, and made a kind of gulping, snorting sound, spraying Chardonnay across the table.

Val, alarmed at her friend's sudden transformation into a garden sprinkler, shrieked, putting her stubby hands to her face. Before she knew it, she was laughing, too. Proper laughing, it was, shuddering and gasping with those tears which had been threatening to come through all day, finally breaking free and running down her face.

She must have gone on a bit long, though, because when

she finally calmed down, she saw that Sheila was looking at her a bit funny. Not that there was anything unusual in that, mind you. She'd been manoeuvring her into conversational cul-de-sacs and then turning all hoity-toity since the year dot.

"The man *is* dead, Val," she cautioned.

"I know," Val sniffed, "I know that. I wasn't being horrible..." She trailed off, scrubbing at her damp nose with a screwed-up piece of toilet roll.

"Still," Sheila went on, lowering her eyes to show that she, at least, was capable of respect, "I'm sure he would have wanted us to remember him this way."

Under the table Val's foot twitched up and down, pumping an imaginary pedal. Sheila hadn't even been in his class, hadn't even known him! How could she bloody well sit there and say what he would have wanted? And who, in God's name, would want to be remembered as a *leg*?

"I'll tell you what Mr Denny would have wanted," she said, her voice cracking. "He would have wanted to be happy, that's what! Then he wouldn't have had to throw himself under that stupid train!"

She was crying again, but she wasn't exactly sure why, the tears racing down her cheeks like raindrops chasing each other down a windowpane. In truth, she hadn't known anything about Mr Denny either, well, apart from the fact that he played the clarinet and was keen on the Royal Family.

People were always been trying to get him talking in lessons so they that they wouldn't have to do any work. Every week someone would say something like, "When did the Queen come to the throne, Sir?" or, "Do they have a royal family in other countries?"

'The Denster' as they called him behind his back, oblivious to all the whispering and giggling, fringe bouncing up and down emphatically as he spoke, would launch into a monologue which, if they prompted him in all the right places, could last well over half an hour.

She took another tissue out of her handbag and blotted the tears away, knowing it was pointless because she probably looked all puffed-up and puce by now. More or less, she supposed, the same colour as her overalls, which she was still wearing because Sheila had insisted on picking her up straight from work. At least she'd had the good sense to shove the baseball cap out of sight.

"Here," Sheila muttered, pushing the wine bottle towards Val. "You'd better pour yourself another one."

She took it and filled her glass, glugging a big mouthful and trying not to taste it too much. It was so sour that it made the glands at the side of her throat screw themselves up into little balls and she wished she'd been brave enough to ask for a brandy and coke. But this place was all chalk boards and putty-coloured paint and she didn't think they'd look too kindly on her request. They should have gone down the Pawleyne Arms in Penge.

It was alright for Sheila with her new kitchen and her husband having his own business. She'd emigrated to Chislehurst and had her 'colours done'. She could sit there in her peach, cashmere wrap, confident that the shade brought out the best in her skin tone. Who was going to want to listen to a purple woman in a purple safari suit talking about her flat above the newsagent and her ex-husband's haemorrhoids?

"So, this hairdresser," Sheila began again, tilting her head to one side and arranging her features into an expression she usually used when talking to people who were recuperating after a long illness. "He said purple..."

"Aubergine," Val corrected.

"...he said it was a good idea, did he?"

"Actually, he said it spoke of Nature's bounty, fine wine and sun-ripened fruits," Val answered, sticking her chin out like an ironing board. "I think it suits me."

She ran her fingers through her aubergine thatch, fluffing up the fringe to emphasise the point. She didn't mention that her son, as he'd left for work that morning, had told her she looked like the Great Grape Ape.

A man shuffled up to the table clutching a plastic carrier bag. He had standard-issue grey hair and silver-rimmed bifocals, but his face looked like his mind was preoccupied with all manner of terrible Technicolor events that might kick off at any minute. "Clissold Grange? Penge?" he asked, glancing from Sheila to Val and back again.

Sheila responded to the password by extending her hand. "It certainly is. Glad you could make it. Sheila Rumbold and Valerie Inchworth." She paused, waiting to see if the names triggered any response in the man. When none was forthcoming, she continued, "Please take a seat. We're expecting quite a few."

"Terry Freeman. Pleased to meet you," the man answered, sitting down and looking intently at the table.

Three more people joined the table, two women and a man. Val didn't catch their names and although she didn't recognise them, as such, they looked vaguely familiar. Mind you, she pondered, when you got to her age, everyone looked as if you might have met them before.

Silence settled for a moment. Sheila piped up, "Wasn't it terrible about poor Mr Denny?" and they all murmured agreement. Who would have thought that being a French teacher was so stressful, someone commented. Someone else said that they'd been in his class and he'd always appeared cheerful. Terry stared at the table some more and muttered that he wasn't surprised, wasn't surprised at all.

Val twiddled a little vase holding a single, acid green flower, the like of which she'd never clapped eyes on before. Probably genetically engineered, she shouldn't wonder. When a waitress arrived, all young and long-limbed, pale and smooth and straight as a plank of Scandinavian wood, Val wondered whether her name was 'Ikea' and whether someone had tampered with her DNA, too. They were all like that in here with their shirts and ties and buttoned-up waistcoats, give or take a hairdo.

Val pulled at her jacket, which was too tight across the bust and whose man-made fibres were giving off the scent of unleaded four-star. Looking at them all sitting here round the table, it was difficult to believe any of them had ever looked like these shop dummies in their youth.

As for herself, she could hardly remember a time when she hadn't had these two great puddings stuck on the front of her chest, making her look huffy and indignant even when she wasn't. Caused her no end of trouble, they had, over the years and now there was her boss, Mr Khan, and his dodgy magazines and—

"I said 'dancing'. Isn't that right, Val?"

"Sorry?" she said.

"And then she found out she had to go topless, didn't you, Val?" Sheila cackled. "Imagine that!"

She should have guessed that Sheila would whip out her get-out-of-jail-free card. She always did after a couple of glasses. Tonight, though, Val wasn't in the mood to play the good sport and the words 'sod' and 'off' were beginning to form in her mouth. But before she could speak, she was distracted by a bunch of keys which one of them had plonked on the table.

Attached to the key ring was a small, enamelled disc glued onto a little, leather flap which looked like a dog's ear. The words 'Isle of Man' circled an emblem showing three emerald green legs, joined together at the top, knees bent, running furiously round in a circle, going nowhere.

Val's tears were ready to overflow again. "Sorry," she whispered, pushing the chair back with a honking sound and hurrying outside.

In the courtyard the air was cool as dusk came down. A pigeon strutted past, looking for crumbs. A police siren screeched in the distance. Lights snapped on in windows across the way.

She perched on a bench and reached into one of her pockets – at least bloody safari suits weren't short on those – and pulled out a small, black box. Taking out a thin, white cylinder like a stick of chalk, she pressed a button on the side and put it to her lips. She began to feel more relaxed and her warm, salty, tear-tightened skin made her imagine she'd spent the day on a beach instead of at the petrol station.

"That one of those e-cigarettes?" asked a voice beside her.

Val turned and saw a man leaning against the wall, arranging little tufts of tobacco along a cigarette paper. He had a small, round, symmetrical face and thin, grey hair pulled back into a straggly pony tail which looked like a clump of something a person might pull out of a bath plug hole.

"That's right," she answered.

A laugh spluttered out of the man making his shoulders heave. "What are you doing out here, then?"

She knew full well he was taking the piss but she didn't much care. "Old habits, I suppose," she shrugged. "And it gives me an excuse to get away, doesn't it?"

"Got a 'do' on?" he asked, tilting his head towards the bar.

His eyes were soft with half-moon eyelids. With his thin neck and long, padded coat he reminded her of a kindly tortoise.

55

"One of those internet things," she shuddered. "Idiots Reunited, or something. I didn't want to come."

"Why would you?" said the man, straightening up and speaking more forcefully. "Ghosts. They're all ghosts. Shadows from the past. What are you gonna say to ghosts?" He opened his arms and let them flop back to his sides.

"Nah," he shook his head, carrying on. "Doesn't do to go back. Fair enough if you could turn up and say you've made a million quid or you're married to a supermodel but how many of us can do that? I used to want to be a musician," he went on. "I can play the guitar, carry a tune."

He looked away, puffing on his roll-up and thinking his own thoughts. "Life took other turns," he added, as if to himself.

Val wondered whether she'd made a mistake talking to the man. He'd looked alright but a person's mood could change like the flick of a switch, she knew that.

"What about you?" he looked at her again.

"How do you mean?" she asked. She couldn't play an instrument, if that's what he was getting at.

"Dreams. Ambitions," he said. "What did you want to do?"

Val was hot and flustered again. Where to begin? She'd wanted the same things as everyone else, she supposed. Her curls trembled as she spoke. "I... well. Nice car, travelling, my own house. I wanted to learn to ice skate for a while and then it was horse riding," she explained. "But if you mean proper ambitions, I suppose I hoped I would be a dancer. I wanted to go to Paris and be a Bluebell Girl. But, let's not get into that. Like you say, life takes other turns. But I also used to have this idea, silly, I know, of driving a milk float for a day," she went on. "In fact, I'd forgotten all about that one till I was in the hairdresser's the other day."

She'd blathered on too much, she knew, and she

regretted necking all that wine. "Button it, Val," was what her husband used to say. She peered in through the window. Maybe it was time to re-join Sheila and the others.

But the friendly tortoise man started chuckling again. "You're kidding!" he said. He threw his cigarette on the ground and stamped on it. "Come with me!"

He grabbed her wrist and before she could pull away, he was dragging her down the street.

"Wait!" she protested, half wailing, half giggling. "Where are we going? I can't just leave like this."

Round the corner, they dipped into a side street. A little further down he suddenly stopped and swung round to face her. "Your carriage awaits, m'lady," he announced in a plummy voice, bending low like he was going to sling his padded coat over a puddle.

Val peeped over his shoulder and saw a milk float parked at the side of the road. "How do you mean?" she said.

"You wanted to drive one, didn't you?"

"Yes, but..."

"Well, jump in!"

They clambered onto the seat which was more like a bench. It was cold through Val's trousers.

"Shunt up," he said and she found herself sitting in front of the steering wheel.

"But I can't... I've never..." she protested but he just smiled and dangled a set of keys in front of her face.

"When are you gonna to do it if you don't do it now?" he asked.

He reached behind him and picked up a grubby, peaked cap, like a sailor might wear, and plonked it on Val's plum-coloured cranium. "Gotta look the part."

The hat was heavier than it looked and kept slipping over her eyes but Val put the key in the lock and pressed down gently on the pedal, like he told her to. The float lurched forwards and she shrieked, terrified of the sensation of movement. Slowly, very slowly, they pulled away from the kerb. It reminded her of riding the dodgems at the fairground.

"Gently does it…" The Milkman warned, grabbing the wheel and steering them away from a parked car. "You treat her nicely, she'll treat you nicely."

Val manoeuvred the float down another side street. They were barely going ten miles an hour but she was exhilarated, like she was swishing down the Cresta Run.

On they went, a bit further. She was getting into her stride, now, although she still squealed every time they went over a bump in the road. Sod Sheila and her stupid wine bar! This was more like it!

But then a van turned into the end of the street and made its way towards them. The road was narrow here and, with cars parked either side, someone was going to have to clear out of the way. It didn't look like it was going to be the other driver.

Panicking, Val swerved towards the pavement at exactly the same time that she put her foot down hard on the accelerator.

"Hang about!" The Milkman yelled but it was too late.

The float skidded round in an arc, the back of it hitting a parked car with an almighty, high-pitched crash as the crates of rattling bottles smashed together and tipped out into the street. When Val remembered it all later, she recalled colours and shapes streaking past like the inside of a kaleidoscope. For just a fraction of a moment the float teetered on two wheels as if it might tip onto its side but then it settled itself and bounced to a stop.

Val and The Milkman sat still, not quite trusting that the

action was over. An alarm started wailing and a man rushed out of a house, yelling. Someone called the police.

Eventually, they climbed out, shaken but relieved they hadn't been hurt and sat on the kerb, sipping sweet tea which a neighbour had made them. Although most of the bottles in the float had been empty, a few had had milk in them which was now, Val noticed, trickling down the drain.

At the police station a policewoman escorted them down a corridor and into a square room with a big blue door. Inside there was a table and four chairs but no window and not a single poster on the walls to entertain the eye. They sat down, as directed, and the WPC slipped out the door, closing it behind her.

"Now what?" Val sighed. Couldn't they just tell them how 'naughty' they'd been and let them go? Why did people always have to wait around for hours on end while other people – policemen, doctors, civil servants – filled out stupid forms?

"We could make a break for it," The Milkman shrugged, trying the door handle and finding it was locked. He sat back down.

Val's eyes were tired under the strip lighting. The man looked his age and she guessed she probably did, too. Neither of them had the energy to speak any more and had reverted to being strangers, as if all their high spirits had trickled away with the spilt milk.

After a while, the door opened and a policeman came in holding a clipboard and a mug made in the shape of Prince Charles's face, the ears serving as handles. Val slumped at the table. The Milkman tilted back in his chair, watching.

"Put the chair flat on the floor, there's a good chap," the policeman said. "Now I'm sure I don't have to tell you both that what happened this evening could have had very serious consequences. Very serious indeed."

His accent was posher than Val would have expected but then perhaps she'd seen too many cockney cop dramas on the telly.

The policeman carried on, pacing round the table, shoes squeaking. "Have you considered what might have happened if there had been a child playing in the street? Have you?" His grey hair, which had been combed back, flopped forward, bouncing as he spoke. "What if you yourselves had been injured? I must say, this is the kind of behaviour I would have expected from teenagers, not responsible adults!"

Val glanced at The Milkman and saw that he was still tilting on his chair and trying not to laugh. The policeman, she saw, was glaring at him with small, grey eyes and growing more irritated by the minute.

"Look. I've already asked you to put your chair flat on the floor," he snapped. "The furniture in here is the property of Her Majesty's Government and therefore is to be treated with respect. What you do in your own home with your own furniture is your concern!"

The Milkman sighed and set the chair back down.

The policeman took a pen from his top pocket and clicked it on. "Now," he began, looking at Val. "We'll start with you, shall we? Name and address, if you please."

He lifted his leg up, resting his foot on the edge of the table and balancing the clipboard on his knee.

It was like in the films.

Everything slowed down and all Val could see, close-up and in perfect, microscopic detail, was the policeman's leg. The milk bottle skin. The hairs glinting under the fluorescent light. The slightly-scuffed, regulation, lace-up shoe. She caught her breath. All that was missing from the moment was a soundtrack of angels singing.

Her heart was pounding as she switched her attention to

his face. Yep, the earnest expression was still there, alright, and, she noted, the acne had faded leaving little dents where there had once been purple pustules. It was so bloody obvious. Why hadn't she seen it straight away?

"You're alive!" Val whispered and she didn't know whether to laugh or start sobbing again.

"Of course I'm alive! What on Earth are you talking about?" the policeman barked.

"It *is* you, isn't it?" she said again, putting her hands to her face as the tears spilled over once again.

Constable Denny, it turned out, had left the teaching profession some years earlier looking for a new challenge and was now not far from retirement.

The suggestion that he had thrown himself under a moving vehicle was, he said, preposterous, and he could only surmise that the rumour had come about due to some confusion with Mr Marchmont, the PE teacher, who had indeed, sadly, committed suicide.

This misunderstanding, PC Denny concluded, was one of the drawbacks of using social networking websites, which he hoped those present would note well.

When Val put forward that she had been in his French class, he said gosh and goodness me and nodded, as if he remembered her but she wasn't falling for it. He didn't know her from a bar of soap. With The Milkman, though, it was a different story.

"Now we come to you, my good man. Name and address?"

Val flushed when she realised that she didn't know The Milkman's name, either.

"Dave Crowther," he began.

PC Denny stared at him for a moment. "Wait a minute. Good Lord! You're not...?"

"Yeah, that's right," Dave smirked. "Clissold Grange."

"Well I never!" PC Denny exclaimed. "I knew there was something familiar about you. I have to say that I am disappointed to find you here in such circumstances, though not entirely surprised."

Val sat up like she'd had an electric shock.

"Clissold Grange? You never said!" she gasped. "What about the wine bar... were you...?"

"...OK, OK. I admit it," Dave-The-Tortoise-Milkman lifted his hands in surrender. "I chickened out. Like I say, too many ghosts."

The Denster finally packed them off home with a warning and a cheerful 'au revoir'. As she went down the steps of the station and out into the night, Val felt relieved as well as something else that she couldn't quite put her finger on.

As she passed the wine bar, she peered inside. The staff were putting chairs on tables and mopping the floor. Sheila would be furious and who could blame her? Dealing with her would be tomorrow's problem. The street was empty and after looking carefully from side to side, Val pirouetted the length of the pavement, twirling round and round until she reached the corner, laughing and breathless.

When she got home, she noticed she was still holding The Milkman's hat.

Don't Forget The Suncream

Maureen had never been too keen on animals. Too much noise and mess and she didn't see why she should change her opinion now. But she didn't want that wiry, little goat of a man in the vest and khaki shorts going on about the 'Poms' again, so she held out her hand and winced.

They were like that over here. It was all 'The Biggest' this or 'The Best' that, like the whole bloody nation was working for the Australian Tourist Board.

And that bridge! There were hundreds of the things going over the Thames but you didn't hear the British banging on about them, did you? As for the Opera House, it looked like an upturned, polystyrene, fast food container. No, there was plenty of top-notch scenery back in England, thanks very much, as anyone who had seen the sun set over Great Yarmouth would tell you.

Still, Maureen had been absolutely certain that she needed to come here, though she couldn't say why, exactly. She'd had her hair done, fallen asleep under the drier and when she woke up, she'd gone straight to the travel agent in the High Street.

Melvin had stared at her, gob hanging open, when she told him she was going and who could blame him? The furthest she'd ever been was a day trip to Calais. Then again, maybe it was her new, blue barnet that had put the wind up him.

But perhaps it wasn't so irrational. When she thought about it, Australia had always been there, hovering in the doorway of her mind. She just hadn't noticed it before.

At school there had been a big chart on the wall showing a map of 'Australasia', as they called it, and the animals and birds which inhabited it. Strange animals they were, with pouches and beaks in odd places and birds with bright plumage and rattling calls. She used to like looking at it and she remembered thinking that the koalas looked a bit like Mr Peascroft, the history teacher.

One Christmas she overheard her mother murmuring something about convicts being sent Down Under. She used to wonder if that was where her dad had disappeared to and after that, she scrutinised the poster more closely, looking in vain for men in suits with arrows, lurking in the vegetation.

And years later, a woman she worked with used to bring in postcards every week from her son who was travelling there with a group of friends. She was full of it all. "Oh, my Steven's in Sydney this week!" at the top of her voice. But on the quiet, Maureen used to look forward to her reading them out. Each card was full of some new adventure and you could really feel the boy's excitement. There had been a lot of peculiar place names, 'Woollomoloo' and 'Geelong'. Like joke names, really.

The man in the vest made a clicking noise with his tongue. "Come on, mate," he coaxed. "Just take it from the lady's hand… They're shy creatures, y'see," he went on, turning to the visitors gathered round him. "You've just got to—"

Maureen shrieked, jumping back. Put its nose right up against her, it had, all cold and wet like a packet of frozen peas.

"Strewth!" the man laughed, fiddling with his ear, as if she'd deafened him. "It's only a wallaby! Thought you Poms were a nation of animal lovers!"

Everyone tittered but Maureen was furious. She'd let the side down and she could have kicked herself, she really could, or, rather, kicked that man. Doug must have seen the look on her face because he put a hand on her shoulder and steered her towards the café.

"Come on," he chuckled. "Let's go and have a brew."
They walked along the rusty-looking path, past the emu enclosure and the kangaroos, back to the ticket booth. There was a kiosk there selling refreshments and Maureen sat down at a wooden table in the shade of a tall, scabby-looking tree while Doug went to get some drinks.
Other tourists were dotted around at other tables, Swedes, Germans, maybe, and other Brits, most of them young and dressed holiday-style in baggy T-shirts, shorts and fluorescent sunglasses. Flip-flops, as well, though the locals called them 'thongs'. Nearly choked, she had, the first time she'd heard that.
Maureen couldn't go that far but she had bought herself a pair of loose, cotton trousers in a tropical print. Very comfortable they were, though she still wore them with tights underneath. After all, you had to keep your standards up.
Doug came sauntering back, flip-flops clacking lazily against his feet. He sat down opposite her, sliding a tray onto the table.
"There you go, Mo," he said, pushing a cup towards her, adding, "Hey, that rhymes, doesn't it?"
Normally she put people straight when they called her Mo but with him she didn't mind.
They'd got talking at the airport. She had never been on a plane before and it wasn't at all how she imagined it. It was loud and crowded, for one thing, much like being on the 358 bus for twenty-four hours.
They'd served up food on trays with diddy little compartments containing different things, like edible advent calendars. But Maureen had brought her own sandwiches. You never knew who'd prepared things, did you? Besides, the salad had a black olive in it.
Thank the Lord, then, for Doug. He'd seen her

struggling with her suitcase and come over to help. He had a great big guide book, thick as a phone directory, and he brought her to Bluey's Hostel (she had to laugh at the name). He showed her the ropes – the showers were only hot in the mornings and though you could wash your clothes in the communal laundry, if you left them to dry they'd be nicked. It was best to use the kitchen early if you were cooking, he warned. Leave it too late and all the pots and pans would be piled up and filthy.

Maureen thought it was a liberty, charging good money for such shoddy facilities but Doug told her she'd get used to it.

She wasn't so sure. She liked things clean and scrubbed. She liked air fresheners and furry toilet seat covers, not ashtrays full of fag butts and treading in other people's urine because they were too drunk to aim at the lavatory bowl. But she'd been there a week now and had to admit she was learning to tolerate the slapdash nature of communal life.

And what with the blue hair, people seemed to think she was more relaxed than she really was. Anyway, she pondered, sometimes you get tired of being yourself. You want to play a different role for a change.

A dingo howled in the distance. Probably had enough of that blasted man, too, she shouldn't wonder. Doug slurped at a bowl of noodles while Maureen drank her tea. She had never seen anyone scoff so much food and stay so thin. He was tall and pale with it, too, like a willow twig stripped of its bark, and he wore a big, knobbly, silver ring on one of his thumbs and a little bracelet on his wrist made of plaited threads.

But that wasn't the half of it. The boy had a tablecloth wrapped round his waist.

Maureen had spotted it soon as he turned up that

morning but she'd said nothing. Now she could hold back no longer. She shook her head, her olive green eyes darting from side to side with indignation. "I just don't know how you can go round in... that," she said.

Doug scooped a spoonful of noodles into his mouth. "It's a sarong," he shrugged. "They wear them all the time in Asia."

"But it's a skirt!" she gasped. The idea of Melvin done up like that would be enough to put anyone off their cornflakes.

Doug burst out laughing, almost spraying the table. "Try saying that to a Scotsman!" he spluttered. "Anyway," he went on, "what's wrong with it? Women wear trousers."

He was a bit like that. Always taking her up on her opinions. It made a change. If Maureen was honest, she got fed-up of people at home agreeing with her for a quiet life. Sometimes she wanted to shake Melvin, she really did, when he said, "Whatever you say, my love."

Back in the UK Doug had worked with homeless people or psychiatric patients. Something like that, anyway, and he knew how to slide things into the conversation a bit crafty, like. "Why do you say that?" he would say, or, "Can you explain that a bit more?" Sometimes he just laughed at her and shook his head.

When they'd finished eating and drinking, they went out through the turnstiles and back onto the road. Maureen couldn't remember the name of where they were, something with a 'bingbong' or an 'idgee' in it, not that it was much of a town, anyway. More like a collection of garden sheds.

The beach was just a short walk away on the other side of the road. They crossed over and took off their shoes, labouring through the sand till they reached the line of froth where the ocean came in and the ground was firmer.

The water was a beautiful colour, she had to admit, just like in the holiday brochures, with clean-looking sand and not a discarded plastic bag in sight. A couple of teenagers were kicking a ball around but, apart from them, there was no-one else to be seen.

"Don't you feel strange hanging about with someone my age?" she asked Doug, suddenly. "It must be like going around with your mother!"

"I get on really well with my ma," he shrugged. Maureen had never met anyone who called his mother 'ma' before.

"She's divorced," he went on. "I'd love to see her doing what you're doing, Mo. You know, dyeing her hair, just taking off, forgetting all her troubles. At the moment she…"

He tailed off, waggling his hand to indicate someone lifting a glass to their lips. He looked down and scratched his toe across the wet sand, making a zigzag pattern. Maureen noticed a fine coating of fair hair on his chin catching the sun. Trying for a beard, no doubt.

Doug's silly mother, whoever she was, wanted telling. She ought to be proud of him, not boozing herself into a stupor! Maureen knew only too well what it was like living with a soak.

Seized with an urge to lift the mood, she took out her phone.

"Come on," she ordered. "Let's be having you."

Doug obliged with a zany pose, spreading his arms, opening his mouth wide and belting out the tune to an ice cream advert. If she'd seen someone doing that in Penge High Street, she'd have tutted and rolled her eyes. Now, on the other side of the world, she laughed so much, she almost sprang a leak.

Doug snatched the phone. "Your turn."

Maureen posed, hands on hips, legs astride with the weight on the balls of her feet, like the netball captain she had once been. "What's so funny?" she demanded as he tried in vain to supress a laugh.

"Your hair!" he sniggered. "It's, like, camouflaged against the sky!"

They strolled over to some smooth, grey rocks at the far end of the bay and sat down together on a boulder.

"How about you? Got any kids, Mo?" he asked.

Well, she certainly hadn't seen that one coming. She looked out across the sea. The sunlight made a pretty picture, bouncing little flecks of light off the water although as she stared, the scene began to get a bit blurry.

"No," she said, and then, "...well," the frown line like a knife nick between her eyes.

So she told him about the August wedding. Nothing fancy. Just family and a few friends at the local Methodist church. A dreadful building, all ornamental concrete and funny angles, but they'd picked it because it was the nearest to where they lived. She'd never been one for all that religion but afterwards she used to sit in there sometimes just for the quiet.

Her dress had been plain, ending just above the knee and she wore it with a little, square jacket and her mother's pearls for 'something borrowed'. Melvin looked sharp in a new suit, though she wasn't going to tell him that, and he kept straightening his cuffs and picking imaginary bits of fluff off his lapels.

Uncle Peter gave her away ('something old,' Melvin joked) and she carried lilies but, wouldn't you know it, they wilted before the service even began. Bloody typical! Melvin had ordered them from someone he knew down the market. When they came out of the church, Maureen whacked him over the head with the half-dead bouquet and someone took a picture. His brother Alf had called out something about rolling pins and everyone laughed. And, after a few sandwiches and sausage rolls in the church hall, that was that. Married life.

She fell pregnant within a year. She'd always been as regular as clockwork so she knew straight away but she lost the baby within three months. Because it was early on, people seemed to think she shouldn't mind too much. They didn't want to see her sorrow. It made them uncomfortable. Everyone wanted her to be tough-old-boots Maureen, like she normally was. But when she was on her own, she wept buckets.

But it kept on happening. Every time it was like one more layer of grief was built up, like another coating of tough, weatherproof varnish. She stopped crying, even when she was on her own, because she worried that once she started, she might not be able to stop.

But one poor little so-and-so made it a bit further. Seven months, she carried him. They called him William, after her father, and after that they stopped trying.

Melvin was no bloody use, was he? Once or twice, he came into the bedroom when she was sitting staring out of the window. Looking at the sky, watching the clouds morphing into different shapes, made her feel calm. He used to walk in the room, clear his throat and walk out again. She wanted to hurl a bottle of cough syrup after him.

Doug listened to her talk without saying anything at all. When she had finished, he said, "It must have been very painful," and squeezed her hand.

"Yes," she replied and felt the loosening in her chest of a knot she hadn't realised was there.

It was almost time to get back to the coach. "You go ahead," she told Doug. "I'll be along in a minute."

After he'd gone Maureen sat for a while looking at the

sea. She wondered what time it was in Penge and whether Melvin was remembering to put the rubbish out. She stood and clambered across the rocks, feet slithering on the dusting of loose sand, almost going over on her ankle, until she stood on the highest one, overlooking the ocean.

She glanced behind her. No-one could see her from the road, she was sure of that. She took off her sandals and, quick as she could, stepped out of her trousers. And then, under the Australian sun, Maureen Bristow did something unthinkable. She took off her 50-denier, tan-coloured, nylon tights and hurled them into the ocean.

A breeze caught them and for just a moment they were carried into the sky, the flailing legs making the shape of the letter W although it could have been an M, before they dropped quickly from sight into the waves.

After she'd put her trousers and shoes back on, Maureen stood a moment longer looking at the coastline curving into the distance. She couldn't remember whether she was looking towards the city or away from it. Perhaps it didn't matter. The sea scuffed half-heartedly at the rocks below, carrying on as if nothing had happened.

When she got back to the bus stop, Doug was waiting by the coach.

"OK?" he asked.

"Yes," she agreed. "All OK now."

They sat in silence as the coach rumbled back to the city. Maureen looked out the window at the darkening sky, wondering what strange creatures were lurking in the scrub at the side of the road. Doug dozed, his head lolling onto her shoulder.

The following morning Maureen was sitting in the courtyard outside the hostel. It was still quite early in the day but pleasantly warm with a gentle breeze rustling the eucalyptus leaves.

71

A loud type from New Zealand was braying at a short, blonde, northern girl telling her about how much beer he'd consumed when he'd been in the outback shearing sheep. The girl must have been impressed because she was competing with tales of her own excesses. Why on Earth did these women feel they had to keep up, Maureen wondered. What happened to being ladylike?

She'd bought a postcard showing a cartoon of a koala drinking a can of beer which she planned to send to Melvin. 'Hic! from Down Under,' it said. But what to write? In all the years they'd been married, she'd never sent her husband novelty stationery.

She looked up and saw Doug coming towards her. This time he was wearing a baggy, olive-green T-shirt and cut-off jeans and had a huge backpack strapped on like a turtle shell. She knew he was leaving today for the Great Barrier Reef (it would have to be 'Great', wouldn't it?) to meet some friends from university and go scuba diving, but hadn't expected he would be departing this early in the day.

He grinned and hugged her with his long, thin arms, "Well, this is it," he smiled. "Here, I've got you something." He took her arm and tied a little, plaited, pink and red ribbon onto her wrist.

"What's this for?" she asked.

"It's a friendship bracelet," he replied.

Maureen wanted to say thank you but when she opened and closed her mouth, no sound came out at all. It was quite peculiar.

"Enjoy yourself, Mo and take care," he waved as he walked away, hoisting his bundle onto his back. "It's been a blast. I'll send you a postcard."

He reminded her of a young lad off to school for the first time and at that moment, Maureen hoped, more than anything in the world, that he would be alright.

When she finally re-engaged her voice, it came out raucous, like one of those ridiculous kookaburras. "Don't forget the sun cream!" she called. But it was too late. Doug was gone.

Faking It

The humming noise faded as the dryer came to a stop and the room was hot, still and silent as a desert with a faint heat haze where the warm air had been. Steve rubbed his eyes and yawned. He'd almost dropped off there.

Bunce, the posh geezer with the sideburns, came over. "Allow me," he said, lifting the hood and clicking his heels together. "If Sir would kindly step this way."

He led Steve to a padded chair on the other side of the room and gestured for him to sit down.

"So what does Sir have in mind today?" he asked, looking at Steve in the mirror and resting his hands on his shoulders. "A new colour? Style? A Mohican, perhaps? Not many men of your vintage could carry it off, but you, I think, have the necessary 'je ne sais quoi'."

He flourished his hand in the air as he spoke as if he were playing a set of invisible castanets.

"Well, I dunno…" Steve hesitated.

He wasn't sure if 'je ne sais quoi' was French for 'thick hair' but he knew a man of his age was lucky to have any at all. He'd watched over the years as his friends had combed over and cropped short as their locks thinned out and receded. Barry from the snooker club, for example, with his pock-marked scalp on display, looked like a grapefruit these days.

But his own hair hadn't budged an inch since the last century. Every morning since he was about fifteen, he'd dragged the comb in a mudguard shape above his ears and slicked a crest on top with a flick of his wrist, secretly proud that he had something other men envied.

He cleared his throat, an idea coming together. "The thing is, it's like this. I want to be…"

An image came to mind. A figure walking onto a stage in a cloud of dry ice, the audience cheering and whooping.

74

"Tonight, ladies and gentlemen, I am going to be Steve Actual."

Now that he'd blurted it out, he felt a bit of a plonker and he could see in the mirror see that his cheeks were flushing.

He already was Steve Actual, in a manner of speaking. Steve *Hatchell*, to be precise, except no-one had ever, in all his life, managed to get their heads round his surname. To his friends, workmates, neighbours, market researchers, doctors' receptionists and fellow drinkers down the pub, he'd always been 'Steve Actual'. He'd given up getting annoyed about it.

"There's a talent show down the pub. I thought I might, you know, do a turn..." he shrugged. "It's as good a stage name as any."

"Quite so," Bunce enthused. "Now, if I might make so bold, I'm guessing you're looking for a little razzamatazz in the coiffure department?" he continued. "May I suggest short and silver with a pink rinse? Very showbiz."

"Pink? I don't..." Steve faltered.

"Think Stewart Granger dashing round the jungle. Think George Clooney. Think Bruce Forsyth," Bunce continued, "They've all given Nature a little nudge, you know."

"Bruce Forsyth?"

"God rest his soul," Bunce sighed. "But you take my point."

Steve was losing his bottle. He'd come for a change, alright, but he wasn't sure he wanted to go the candy floss route. He'd never hear the end of it at work.

Carole, on the other hand, had enjoyed her makeover here the other week. She'd come home with her hair all bouffed up and dyed the colour of a London bus, announcing that she needed to rediscover her 'inner flame'.

75

The next day she'd gone to her sister's, leaving a note by the kettle. It didn't make sense.

"Shall we? Could we?" Bunce pressed, waving his scissors in the air, snippety-snip.

Steve shrugged. A man had to do what a man had to do, didn't he?

The hairdresser started work and Steve watched with dismay as great, greasy, yellowing chunks of his crowning glory dropped onto the floor. Seeing it discarded there, he had to admit it looked a bit like the stuff he'd used to lag his boiler.

He remembered the book he'd been reading, one that Carole had left lying around. 'Denizen of the Dunes' was the true story of a female explorer who had shocked Victorian society by wearing trousers and travelling across North Africa on a camel. She'd been the daughter of a vicar and brought up in comfortable surroundings but had given it all up to live in a tent with a nomadic tribesman.

It wasn't the sort of book he would normally have chosen but what with Carole going off like that, he was looking for answers. True, she'd only gone as far as Luton on public transport, but even so.

The woman in the book was described as 'spirited' and had turned her back on traditional feminine pursuits. Carole, on the other hand, had always gone in for that sort of thing. Only the other week she'd got hold of a few twigs with berries on, some of those flowers with tufty heads and a bit of greenery and displayed them in a jug on the dining room table.

She'd asked him what he thought. "Haven't we got any proper vases, then?" he said and she'd looked at him a bit funny.

When that baking show was on the telly, she'd gone into Cake Mode. Her first project had been a plate of éclairs though, as he pointed out, they'd come out more like rock buns.

Next she tried making the Leaning Tower of Pisa out of gingerbread after the contestants on the programme had attempted something similar. The biscuits had come out a bit black round the edges and when she tried to glue them all together with icing, everything collapsed in a heap within minutes. Dear, oh dear, that gave him a good laugh!

Bunce daubed a white paste onto Steve's cranium. "So you're something of a performer, then?" he quizzed. "Or is it just a secret ambition?"

"I can hold a tune, I suppose," he answered. On the quiet, he'd always fancied himself as Penge's answer to Dean Martin. He'd serenaded the loofah in the shower many times but until now, he'd never really thought about doing it in public.

"I just want to surprise the missus," he went on. "Show her what I can do. She's gone a bit over-emotional, hasn't she? A bit doolally."

"Absolutely unfathomable, most women," Bunce commiserated. "But as the great Oscar Wilde once said, 'Women are made to be loved, not understood'."

"Keep 'em on their toes," was what Steve's old man had advised him long ago and he'd taken note of those words. Put in a lot of effort over the years, he had, to stop things going stale. Until now, he'd always believed Carole was happy enough.

The first time he'd laid eyes on her, he knew she was someone he wanted to impress. It was a bank holiday weekend and he was at an air show out in the countryside. She'd walked past with a friend, all fresh and ironed-looking in a candy-striped dress with a cardigan draped over her shoulders, as the girls used to wear them in those days. Her red hair was pulled back into a ponytail which swayed to and fro as she walked.

Steve was with another girl at the time; he couldn't even remember her name now, but she'd been chattering on about this and that, trying to get his attention, but he wasn't listening. He was watching Carole. He knew she'd clocked him, too, because her eyes kept flicking across when she thought he wasn't looking.

When they started to move away, he bolted after her. Normally he had no trouble talking to girls but when Carole turned to look at him with her blue eyes and her nose, small and pink like a gerbil's, all he could manage was 'Hello' and his voice cracked as he said it.

She looked him up and down. "Is that the best you can do?" she asked but she was laughing as she said it.

"No," he said, taking a cigarette out from behind his ear and lighting it. "I'll take you out some time, if you like, and show you."

Carole's friend nudged her in the ribs and sniggered.

He'd bought his first car not long before, a baby blue Zephyr, and he used to spend his weekends washing and polishing it. When he picked her up in it, she laughed, "It's not very big, is it?"

He told her about his job as a carpet fitter and she said, "Eileen's boyfriend works in a bank."

He bought her daffodils and she said she preferred chrysanthemums.

Steve felt like one of those birds where the male has to make several nests for the female to choose from before she will agree to being his mate.

But one night they went to a dance. It was a Halloween party in a local hall and everyone was in fancy dress. Carole had gone as some kind of vampire in a black cape with little trickles of blood drawn at the corners of her mouth. Steve

78

had painted his face green and drawn stitches across his forehead. Didn't tamper with his quiff, though. Some things were sacred.

It had been a jolly enough do. He had a couple of pale ales and Carole drank snowballs. They did a bit of dancing. Halfway through the evening, the sister of a fella he'd been at school with came lurching over in a mummy costume, obviously plastered, and cackled in Carole's face in a sinister way. Carole shoved her away and then the girl turned to him, asking him to dance. He shook his head but she insisted, becoming quite shrill.

People started turning round to look so Steve got up with her, just to shut her up, but they hadn't been dancing long when she slumped against him, arms round his neck, eyes rolling shut. Unsure what to do, he started shuffling towards the side of the hall, dragging her along, thinking he might be able to plonk her in a chair. But before they got there, he tripped over the bandages trailing from her legs and they both went sprawling to the floor, him on top of her, knocking chairs and tables over in the process and making a racket.

Carole had seen it all from where she was sitting and stormed off to the toilet, bolting herself inside. It took Steve near enough the rest of the evening to persuade her to come out and when he finally convinced her there had been nothing going on with the drunken girl, she was meek as a kitten. Kissed him on the cheek and went quietly into the house when he dropped her off.

As for Steve, he experienced a completely new sensation as he made his way home that night. It was if he'd become a bit taller or his lungs were taking in more air, a kind of human hovercraft. Thinking about it some more, it all came down to trousers – he was the one wearing them at last.

So when Carole mentioned the incident the next day, he didn't defend himself quite so insistently. He said the right words, no mistake – all completely innocent, nothing to worry about. But as he spoke, he made the tone of his voice just a *little* bit more matter-of-fact. Let a bit of doubt seep in.

He proposed not long after that and they were married a couple of months later. Everything went well enough at first and then it was like she was taking him for granted, telling him to wear a shirt at the breakfast table, giving him lists of jobs she wanted doing.

So he tried a little experiment.

"My brother says Diane MacCall was asking after me," he said one evening, as casually as he could, without looking up from his newspaper. He'd taken Diane out a couple of times in years gone by and Carole knew that full well. She was folding clothes at the time and had her back to him. She didn't say anything but he saw her shoulders stiffen.

And so it went on. Whenever she was getting too bossy or her mind was on other things, he'd start staying out after work or coming back smelling of 'Nuit D'Amour'. Most of the time he was down the pub with the lads and the perfume was something he kept in a drawer at work for such eventualities, but it worked. Words would be had, followed by reconciliations when it always seemed she was trying a bit harder to be nice to him.

Later on, he became more inventive. He left mysterious letters written on lilac-coloured notepaper lying around. Sometimes, he let Carole overhear him on the telephone, arranging a date, although he was only talking to the speaking clock.

But his latest stunt, the knickers, had been a masterstroke, even if he said so himself. Marital gold dust. He'd found them in the pound shop, yellow, nylon, so baggy you'd need braces to keep them up and embroidered with the words 'Kiss Me Quick!'.

Sure enough, Carole had come across them in his coat pocket last week and gone berserk. There had been tears, recriminations and reassurances and that night he'd got his favourite dinner, sausage and mash.

Surely it wasn't them that had sent her packing, was it?

Rinsed and blow-dried, Steve sat once more in front of the mirror looking at his revised reflection. His hair looked much shorter and cleaner, it was true, maybe even a bit more modern. But there was no mistaking the sugary, pink tint to his new style. He looked like a Christmas fairy.

"It's taken decades off you," Bunce enthused, wafting a halo of hairspray across his creation. "However, a word to the wise," he lifted the tinted specs from Steve's face. "Ditch these. Far too 'seventies."

As Steve left, Bunce bowed low. "Knock 'em dead, My Liege, and remember, 'Faint heart never won fair lady'."

A week later, Carole made her way down Penge High Street, anxious to reach the pub before the rain started again. Already the pavements were giving off that wet-dog-and-cardboard aroma that she loathed and she couldn't abide the idea of her feet slithering around in damp sandals.

She caught sight of her ketchup-coloured hairdo in a shop window as she passed and pulled herself up a little straighter. The hairdresser had been right, it *did* reflect something of her passionate side. There were rumours that her grandmother had been part Spanish. Who was to say that some of those feisty, Latin chromosomes hadn't found their way through to her?

Her hair had been red when she was younger but had faded over the years to a kind of sandstone shade. Now, with the colour intensified once more, it was like the volume had been turned up on her life, too. Luton wasn't the Costa del Sol but it was something different, at least.

When she reached the venue, she hesitated before going in. In all the years she'd lived in Penge, she'd only ever been in there once or twice. It wasn't really her kind of place. She much preferred taking a drive out to the country, to a village pub where they had a real fire and people smoked pipes and brought their dogs and said 'Good evening' to each other. Still, Steve had begged her to come, so here she was. She wasn't staying, though. He needn't think that.

As the door creaked open, Carole saw exactly what she'd been expecting inside. Red, velvet seating, heavy, wooden furniture, dartboard, congealed carpet and an assortment of disillusioned-looking drinkers dotted around the gloom, all staring into the distance. At the far end of the bar was a small stage with speakers either side and a bank of coloured lights flashing slowly on and off like they couldn't be bothered.

"Are you here for the talent show?" asked a young man in a white shirt with a cheerful voice, popping up in front of her. "Pound a ticket."

Carole took one, bought herself a large port and squirrelled herself at a small table some distance from the stage, taking care not to catch anyone's eye.

This, she supposed, was the 'surprise' Steve had mentioned. Typical! No doubt she'd have to gasp and clap, tell him he was wonderful. Couldn't the man, just for once, buy her a bunch of flowers and a box of chocolates? Couldn't he compliment her on *her* hair or *her* outfit?

For years, she'd gone along with the phoney love letters and the cheap scent and the boasts of the women who'd given him the eye. She'd acted outraged at the furtive phone calls, never letting on that she'd listened on the extension and knew full well it was the speaking clock.

82

She knew he was looking for some kind of fuss to be made, so feeling sorry for him, she'd churned out one Oscar-winning performance after another, wailing and weeping, pleading with him to stay, telling him she loved him. It was like humouring a child, but then, her mother had warned her before she got married that all men were children.

But those enormous, yellow bloomers were absolutely the last straw. Did he really, *really* believe she was going to fall for that? He'd even left the price tag on! It was an insult.

Well, no more. She needed to relight her fire, as those nice boys in that pop group used to sing, and she'd gone to Luton to do so. She'd had enough of faking it.

Someone tapped a microphone and the speakers made a high-pitched screeching sound that hurt Carole's ears. She looked round. More people had come into the pub and it was now quite crowded.

A man with glasses and an anorak, who looked like he'd shuffled in by mistake, stepped onto the stage and welcomed everyone to the pub's first talent contest, promising them an exciting and varied line-up. First on was a pair of teenage musicians, with lank hair dripping onto their guitars, playing a folk number. Out of tune but at least they were trying. Then followed a magician, a Michael Jackson impersonator and an old man playing a mouth organ.

Carole reached into her handbag for her phone, checking the time. She didn't want to be out too late. A man in a pale, pink shirt with pointy collars and sparkly trousers stepped up to the microphone. "This one's for my wife," he rasped, his voice blurred by the sound system. He nodded at someone to the side of the stage, there was a click and a soundtrack of violins started up.

"Oh, Carol," he sang in a voice that was surprisingly

high, given his bulk, and tuneful, too. A familiar melody filled the room.

Carole clapped her hands to her mouth. My God! She hadn't been paying attention, hadn't even realised! It was Steve, her own husband! His hair looked so different (pink or was it the lights?) and he wasn't wearing his glasses.

She'd heard him singing in the shower so many times and never taken any notice. In fact, she usually told him to shut up. But there he was, sauntering across the stage, smiling at the audience, voice as mellow as a clarinet. The room was suddenly hot and Carole thought she was going to cry.

Steve completed his song, striking a pose and pointing at the audience as the music finished. "Let's have a big round of applause for Steve Actual!" the anorak man announced and the audience cheered and whistled. Carole wanted to rush over and hug him but held back, suddenly shy like a starstruck teen.

Steve took a bow and edged over to one side of the stage, squinting for the steps down, and when he stumbled a little, a woman came over from behind the bar, offering an arm to steady him. But, blundering about in a world that was unfamiliar and out-of-focus, anxious to find out whether Carole had turned up, Steve stumbled again, going over on one ankle.

This time he toppled off the stage and into the barmaid's arms and crumpled her to the floor like a blade of grass underfoot, flailing around on top of her.

"Ouch!" she snapped. "Mind my back!"

"Sorry, love, sorry," he stuttered.

Some of the audience sniggered. Someone whistled. The compere and a barman rushed over and pulled Steve upright, checking that the barmaid was alright. No harm done.

84

Carole had seen it all from where she was sitting. All the pride she had for her husband slipped away. To think he'd made her come all this way just to humiliate her all over again! No doubt he was expecting her to sob and plead and play the green-eyed, anguished wife for the umpteenth time. It was degrading, that's what it was! She just couldn't do it anymore.

She could feel tears coming again so she snatched her handbag from the table and marched out the door, into the night. The man from her sister's rambling club had invited her to go to walking in the Lake District at the weekend. There was a lovely campsite up there, he said, with posh tents with fireplaces and four-poster beds. 'Glamping' it was called. Carole decided she would go.

Steve dusted himself down and stretched his arms and legs, clicking his joints back into place. What a numpty, staggering off the stage like that! He was still queasy with embarrassment. He frisked his pockets, searching for his glasses and as he put them on, he noticed a blur of red through the frosted glass as the door swung shut.

Up The Workers

Kevin was wheeling his bike out the front door, manoeuvring past bags and shoes and trying not to scrape the paintwork or crack his shins with the pedals.

"Kev?" a voice came sidling down the stairs. "Are you there?"

He clenched his jaw. He could just make a dash for it, say he hadn't heard. Inevitably, he answered.

"Yes, Imogen?" he called, in what he believed to be a carefree manner. Try as he might, he couldn't keep the ecclesiastical tones from his voice.

A young woman appeared on the staircase. She had broad, sinewy, mantelpiece shoulders and her pale hair was wrapped in a brightly-coloured scarf. Large, patterned earrings dangled from her lobes and there was a bolt through her top lip.

"I forgot to mention," she went on. "I've got a couple of people coming over tonight, yeah? So if you could, you know..."

"Understood," Kevin sighed. "Make myself scarce."

It was a good job the public library was open late. He wasn't exactly looking forward to yet another evening sitting in the reference section but as someone who paid his council tax, it was his democratic right to read the newspapers and take advantage of the warmth. It was either that or go to one of the coffee chains and he definitely wasn't giving them his business.

He was about to close the front door behind him when something occurred to him. He turned round for another look at Imogen's outfit. "Er, is that my tracksuit top you're wearing?" he asked.

"This? I found it on a chair," she shrugged. "You don't mind, do you?"

Kevin didn't reply. He closed the door, took a deep breath and pedalled off down the street, reminding himself that possessions were just things. It was a privilege, in a way, to be able to help someone.

Imogen was a friend of someone he worked with and he'd met her when he was running the fairtrade stall at a fundraising event. She'd just returned from volunteering in Africa and when she let slip she needed somewhere to stay, he found himself offering her his spare room for a couple of days. He hadn't expected that she would still be there more than three weeks later, as difficult to get rid of as the mildew on his shower curtain.

He'd tried to ask her about her plans just that morning. "So, Imogen, have you got any work coming up?" he ventured. "You said you might be going to visit your family for a while…"

"Family's *sooo* important," she nodded as she tucked into a second bowl of Kevin's luxury muesli. "In Africa they really know how to look after each other. They've got nothing. Absolutely dirt poor yet they share what they have. You're so lucky to have this," she went on, wafting a limp, olive-skinned arm round the kitchen. "*Sooo* incredibly lucky. But then, I guess it's one of the perks of being a teacher."

Kevin had bristled at that. There was nothing cushy about being a teacher and as for the flat, luck hadn't really come into it. He'd saved for ages for the deposit and even then, he'd only been able to afford this top floor of a scruffy, Victorian terrace in Penge.

The street had yet to be gentrified. Some of the residents had replaced their wooden, sash windows with plastic or metal frames and painted their front doors lurid colours. Front paths and garden walls were crumbling and satellite dishes like giant sucker pads adorned most of the properties.

Even so, he much preferred the area to the more bourgeois parts of London and it was a million miles from the vicarage in Hemel Hempstead. Here he felt himself to be a man of the people, mixing with those from all backgrounds, able to get on with anyone.

Downstairs was an older couple who mainly kept to themselves though Kevin had heard the woman yelling at the bin men on several occasions. Only last week she'd been seen in the street with bright, blue hair and now her husband said she'd gone abroad. Australia, was it? Kevin knew it wasn't his place to judge but it did seem a bit odd.

Two doors down was an Asian family with teenage sons. The boys liked to sit outside in their car, all the doors flung open like the carapace of some huge, flying insect, flooding the street with relentless, pounding music.

There were out there that very day and Kevin slowed down as he cycled past, wobbling slightly. "Afternoon, guys," he called as one of them clambered out of the driving seat without looking, almost knocking him off.

"Oy! Watch it, mate!" the boy yelled, causing Kevin to wobble even more.

This Buddhism thing, Kevin had to admit, wasn't as easy as it looked. It was all very well trying to be tolerant and patient and he got it, he really did, when Stefan, his yoga instructor, explained how desiring things led to unhappiness. Trouble was, sometimes you just wanted to punch people in the mouth.

On his way to the high street, he went past a small parade of shops and stopped to chain up his bike. It was quieter there and, he hoped, there was less chance of it being nicked.

He saw a shop there he hadn't noticed before bearing the name Hairs & Graces. Curious, he cupped his hand to minimise the glare and peered through the front window.

All he could make out was that it was very purple inside. Was it some kind of gift shop or an attempt at a trendy bar? At that moment the door flung open and a tall man with dark, curly hair and cowboy boot-clad legs that bent slightly backwards like boomerangs stood in front of him.

"Good afternoon, Sir!" he boomed in a plummy voice. "May I interest you in a haircut? Two for the price of one, buy now, pay later? While you wait, as it were?"

Kevin hadn't planned one, as such, although it was true that under his cycle helmet, his thick, red curls were looking a little shaggy. And, where he could, he liked to support small, local businesses.

"Er..." he began, not wanting to say yes, exactly, but not wanting to say no and cause offence, either.

"Come on in," the man cajoled. "Feel free to have a look round."

Kevin stepped inside because he couldn't think of a reason not to. As expected, the room was painted purple and there was soft lighting and lots of silvery mirrors and furnishings.

"Very nice," he smiled. What was the etiquette for complimenting someone on the interior of their shop? Now he'd seen it, maybe he could leave. He started moving towards the door.

"Surely you're not going?" the man went on, blocking his path. "'*The time has come, the walrus said, to talk of many things, of shoes and ships and sealing wax, of cabbages and kings.*' Pray, sit down, my good man. Let me furnish you with a hot beverage."

An hour and a half later, Kevin emerged from the salon with his hair shaved at the back and sides and a sizeable, orange quiff like a French baguette jutting out at the front.

The hairdresser had constructed this style when Kevin announced that he wanted to look 'streetwise'. Wearing a cycle helmet was now out of the question. On the other hand, he quite fancied a jaunty, little cap tilted back, urchin-style.

But that wasn't the only thing Kevin wanted. From the moment that dryer had been switched off, long-forgotten wants, wishes, desires and needs, not to mention yearnings, cravings and yens, had been bubbling up to the surface of his mind like the debris from an unblocked drain.

Where to begin?

He stood on the narrow pavement outside the salon, eyes shining like a child contemplating a Christmas stocking. A fresh breeze was blowing and lacy, white clouds streaked across the sky. Penge, in all its glory, struck him as exciting as Manhattan. He'd never been to New York but still, he pictured it as a place where anything might happen.

"I want," he said, rubbing his hands together with glee. "I want… I want… a burger!"

Leaving his bike next to the railings, he marched down to the main road and into a fast food outlet where he ordered a double cheeseburger and fries. He'd read things about their milkshakes being padded out with potato starch but he slurped down a strawberry-flavoured one nonetheless and it tasted bloody good.

Sated, with ketchup on his pale, slightly receding chin, Kevin returned to his bike, unchained it and slung it into a nearby skip. What was the point of doing his bit for The Environment if nobody else did? He wanted a vehicle that ran on petrol – lots of it – maybe a sports car or, better still, a motorbike.

But first, he wanted one of those fancy, designer laptops that he'd always despised. He'd been disturbed by pictures in the papers showing huge piles of toxic waste in the Far East which had been generated by the western world's relentless demand for new technology but, even so, he marched into the supermarket where they were on special offer and bought one along with a new smartphone.

Next on the agenda was a drink. A proper drink – not the real ale he usually went for that tasted like a mixture of vinegar and old tea bags that had been wrung out of some folk singer's beard. No, Kevin wanted a frivolous drink that spoke of excess and expensive adverts featuring beautiful women and young bucks in bootlace ties.

The Pawleyne Arms was a short walk away. That would do. Striding inside he found it largely empty although there were a few customers in overalls or fluorescent jackets idling at the bar or watching the TV.

One old boy in a brown anorak chuckled as he spotted the bicycle clips clamping Kevin's jeans. "Left your horse outside, mate?"

"Get over it!" Kevin sneered and walked up to the bar.

The barmaid greeted him with a friendly smile and asked what he would like.

"Ooh, let's see, now," he mused, sucking air through his teeth. "How about 'Sex on the Beach'? *And* a drink, of course!"

He winked, then guffawed and banged his hand on the bar, in that one moment trashing his decades of polite, respectful, deliberately non-sexist behaviour towards womankind.

The girl raised her eyebrows and moved quickly away. She spent quite some time sorting through a cardboard box of different-sized bottles under the bar and then she disappeared to the kitchen. A man returned in her place carrying a glass of pinkish liquid with a cherry on a stick in it.

"Sex on the Beach?" he asked, sliding the glass towards Kevin. "We ain't got no cranberry, I'm afraid, so I used blackcurrant squash. And a piece of advice," he warned, "Watch yourself around the ladies."

"Fascist!" Kevin muttered under his breath. He swallowed the drink in two gulps and ordered four more which he asked the barman to tip into a pint glass.

As the alcohol began to warm him, a more nebulous 'want' slowly came into focus, one that had, he now knew, been tugging at his sleeve for most of his life.

He'd sympathised with minorities, donated to the underprivileged, minimised his carbon footprint and eschewed racism, sexism, ageism and every other prejudice he could think of. He'd even sold The Socialist Worker outside tube stations. Yet, still, *still*, people regarded him as someone who'd had it easy. A featherweight. And that rankled.

Kevin found himself trying to explain this to a man with a grey moustache who was also leaning on the bar.

"Stefan says we're all suffering," he slurred. "People think I don't... but I do... just because... not Black or from the Third World..."

"Absolutely," the man nodded.

"I mean, I'm part Welsh, for God's sake!" Kevin went on, jabbing himself in the chest, "...terrible time at the hands of the English. Terrible! But does anyone see that?"

He had never actually been to Wales. His great-grandmother, whose maiden name was Jones, had moved to Hertfordshire as a girl. He had toyed, at times, with the idea of adding the name to his own surname with a hyphen. But no doubt people would simply dismiss 'Jones-Frobisher' as posh.

"Nice place, Wales," the man agreed. "They like a sing-along."

Kevin knocked back the last of his cocktail and wished his comrade a good evening with a hearty slap on the back.

What he really wanted, it suddenly became so clear, was clout. Some respect. Put more formally, he wanted gravitas. That madam in his spare room would be a good place to start. He left the pub and set off home, teetering purposefully up the high street and managing to avoid litter bins and lampposts. Letting himself in the front door, he stomped upstairs to his own flat.

He flung open the door to the living room where Imogen sat cross-legged on the floor, smoking a roll-up. The room was lit only by a couple of candles flickering in coloured, glass jars. A mixed-race man in a khaki shirt was strumming on a guitar and another, younger man in wide-legged trousers and a baseball cap sat next to him on the sofa, tapping his knees.

"OK. Let's be having you," Kevin announced, snapping on all the lights like a nightclub bouncer. "Party's over."

"Oh, hi, Kev," Imogen said, squinting through the smoke. "Like the haircut. I thought you wouldn't be back till later, yeah?"

"It's my flat and I can come and go as I like," he said, burping into the back of his hand. "Now come on, you lot. Clear off," he went on, turning to Imogen's guests.

"OK, no need to get heavy, dude!" said the man with the guitar, standing up.

"I thought you were cool with it, Kev," Imogen whined. "You can't go round chucking people out!"

"I've told you. It's my flat and I can chuck out who I want!" Kevin barked. Being unreasonable, he discovered, was actually quite enjoyable. He made a note to try it more often. "Off you go!" he boomed.

"Take no notice of him," the man in the trousers joined in. "He's got a chip on his shoulder. What do you expect? He *is* ginger."

Everyone fell silent.

Kevin was so shocked, he fell backwards onto the sofa like he'd been punched. *Ginger* he'd called him! My God! People had said things over the years – 'Coppernob', 'Ginger Minge', 'Satsuma Bonce' – of course they had, and especially at school, but he'd never taken much notice.

But all along he'd been a bona fide member of a minority, one that was abused and ridiculed and subject to discrimination. He was well and truly oppressed and he hadn't even realised it till now.

Peace washed over him, the kind of feeling Stefan had said people might achieve with meditation. He sat staring into space for a moment and, when he spoke, he was much calmer.

"Get your things together, Imogen," he said. "Leave your keys in the kitchen, please. And the tracksuit top."

Imogen and her friends flicked glances at each other and shrugged. They left the room and after a few minutes of shuffling and clattering in the spare bedroom, they all clomped down the stairs, banging the front door behind them.

Kevin went to the window and watched them disappear down the street in the direction of the railway station. The sun had almost set and the sky was a pale peach colour fading to deep lilac. The Evening Star was beginning to twinkle.

The moral high ground. The view was good.

Proxy

Judith was having that dream again, the one where she and Tony Prince were drinking cocktails on a terrace overlooking the Mediterranean. He was sitting there, all relaxed with his shirt open to the waist and his teeth nearly as white as his slip-on shoes.

"You look great, babe," he smiled, stroking her hair, which was short and blonde, capable yet feminine and quite unlike the grey, hoover bag fluff of her waking life.

But then Mr Bunce, the hairdresser, shook her shoulders and clicked his fingers in her face several times and Tony evaporated.

"Coo-ee! Mrs Riddle!" Bunce called. "Are you with us?"

"Oh, I'm terribly sorry!" Judith jumped, opening her milky blue eyes. "I'm just so tired, I could have slept all afternoon. Still, best get on," she said, picking up her handbag and moving towards the door.

"Whoa, there!" Bunce admonished, placing a firm hand on her arm. "What about the makeover? We've hardly started."

Oh yes. She'd forgotten about that. It was a lovely idea but her sister was expecting her and would worry if she was late. She shouldn't really have come in at all.

"But now you're here it would be a shame to miss the opportunity," Bunce warned. "As that splendid fellow, Etienne de Something-or-Other, once said, you may not pass this way again."

If only that were true, Judith mused. She was up there three, maybe four, times a week. Her daughters were always on at her about it, saying she couldn't carry on like that, but it was alright for them. They didn't know what Auntie Kiki could be like.

Mr Bunce steered her back towards one of the swivel chairs. He had glimpsed, he said, a free spirit beneath her demure exterior. Why not go for the 'pagan goddess' look, he coaxed? Russet extensions entwined with ivy would echo the muses of the Pre-Raphaelite era and make her the living embodiment of the eternal poetry of womanhood.

"Go home, put on a flowing nightie and stretch out on the patio," he advised, "and I guarantee you'll imagine yourself transported to Stonehenge on the solstice."

Appealing as it sounded, Judith couldn't help imagining how all that hair would only get in the way, especially when she had her hand down the U-bend.

What she really wanted, she told him, was something glamorous and blonde like in her dream. Easy to maintain. Most importantly, it had to be the kind of hairstyle that Tony Prince would admire.

Tony was the one who'd seen her through the hours of relentless scrubbing, hoovering and bleaching. With his bouffant hair, reassuring, transatlantic tones and occasional cheeky wink to the camera, he'd convinced her that he alone knew what she was going through. Without him, she might have given up long ago.

He'd also introduced her to a number of gadgets and products that had made her life so much easier. The steam cleaner, for example, with its selection of nozzles for every surface and crevice, had been a bargain at just £149.99 and had done much to reassure Kiki that the germs really were under control.

And that 'St Tropez' handcream, with Mediterranean essences of lavender and olive, had worked a treat on Judith's callouses. When the sign had flashed up on screen that they were down to the last ten, she'd phoned through as quickly as she could and snapped up a pack of three with a free emery board and next-day delivery.

Mr Bunce seemed delighted with this revelation. "What? Me old mate Terry?" he hooted, throwing his head back and clapping his hands together like a performing seal. "Marvellous! That's absolutely priceless!"

"Terry?" Judith queried. "I don't—"

"Ah yes! Tony's real name is Terry Babcock. Believe it or not, we were at drama school together," Bunce explained. "You might not realise this," he went on, lowering his voice, "but he's actually from the Black Country. Used to talk 'loik thiiis'. Always picked to play servants or yokels as a result. Terribly unfair, of course. Never got to show his full range. Still, the boy done good," he concluded. "Those shopping channels pay quite well, I'm told."

Judith sat fiddling with the small gold cross trembling at her throat, thrilled that she had come that bit closer to her idol. On the other hand, hearing about the reality of his life was confusing, like someone had taken a jigsaw apart and reassembled it in the wrong order.

But surely it wasn't all bad? Tony always chatted so easily with all the other presenters, switching from hoovers to hair removers as the situation demanded, introducing a little banter where it was needed. It was difficult to imagine him being sidelined.

Before she could stop herself she'd asked Mr Bunce if he could arrange a meeting with the great man.

Bunce paused, holding his comb mid-air like a magic wand. "You know, I probably could!" he enthused. "What a magnificent notion! I could certainly phone around, see who's still in touch with him. Leave it with me, Mrs Riddle. I'll see what I can do."

When Judith finally left the salon, her hair had been transformed into something yellower and more solid-looking. But inside she was light as a squirt of pine-fresh, anti-grime-and-limescale foam and more optimistic than she had been in months.

Her sister lived ten minutes away on the ground floor of a square, modern, housing association block built of pinky-yellow bricks that looked like corned beef. Judith hurried round there and let herself in.

Inside was gloomy, with vertical blinds, blank walls and functional, teak furniture – more like a solicitor's office than a home. Any knick-knacks or items that might collect dust had long since been dispatched to the charity shop.

"It's me!" she trilled, slightly breathless, struggling out of her skirt and fleece and into her waterproof boiler-suit as quickly as she could. There was a scuffling noise coming from somewhere in the flat.

"So sorry I'm late," she began as she went into the living room, "but… goodness me, Kiki! What on earth has happened?"

Her sister was sprawled on the floor, arms and legs carefully arranged in a kind of swastika shape, a blue cleaning cloth in one hand, a bottle of anti-bacterial spray in the other. She lifted her head a fraction, just enough to catch sight of Judith standing in the doorway.

"Oh. You've had your hair done," she said in a weak, flat voice.

"Never mind that. What happened? Did you pass out?" Judith asked. "Should I call an ambulance?"

"I thought you weren't coming," Kiki whispered. "I couldn't look at the dust on that skirting board any longer."

"But we've discussed this," Judith sighed. "You promised you wouldn't do anything silly. And you know that skirting board is perfectly clean. I only did it the other day."

She hauled her sister to her feet. Together they shuffled towards the sofa, each hanging round the other's neck like exhausted contestants in a Prohibition-era dance-off. Kiki flopped down. "The cushions! Quickly!" she hissed.

When Judith exhaled, it came from the very bottom of her wipe-clean, plastic boots. She went to the kitchen, opened a drawer and came back with a ruler. She measured thirty centimetres from each armrest and placed a cushion either side at that distance, tilting it just a fraction.

Kiki watched carefully, breathing, "Thank the Lord!" when the procedure was complete.

Judith went back to the kitchen and twanged on her rubber gloves. She wiped the already-sparkling hob, swept non-existent dust from behind the fridge and disinfected the pristine work surfaces. After that, she moved to the bathroom to scrub the grouting yet again, floor to ceiling.

Kiki sat in the living room watching a programme about a dodgy builder who had started repairing someone's roof and disappeared with the money. "Don't forget to use the toothbrush!" she called. "You missed a bit yesterday."

Judith slumped onto the toilet seat, feeling ill from the bitter almond smell of bleach. Surely to God she could rest for just a moment? She caught sight of her new, flaxen crop in the mirror, noting that, for the first time in years, she looked very different to her sister. It was a blessed relief.

They were twins, not the same person, as she'd explained to people numerous times over the years. No, she told them when they asked about the fabled bond they supposedly shared – they hadn't married husbands with the same name nor had the same number of children. And no, she didn't suffer mysterious, telepathic pains when Kiki was ill or injured.

Sometimes, though, Judith got the impression that her sister would prefer it if she did. But was it really so wrong that she'd had a happy marriage? Was it such a betrayal that she had children and grandchildren, a tumble dryer and

National Trust membership? Kiki had had offers. She'd had her opportunities, same as anyone else.

She'd always been particular, of course, but since the mystery virus and the chronic fatigue, she'd become obsessive, forever threatening to exhaust herself with twelve-hour cleaning sessions. Whenever Judith tried to suggest a professional cleaner or even, once, a psychologist, she was yanked back on the choke-chain. "Well, if it's too much *trouble* to help out your only sister," Kiki said and, "It's alright for *you* living in the *green belt.*" She talked in italics these days.

Judith recalled that package trip to Spain back in the days when foreign holidays for the masses were a new idea. She and Kiki had got sunburned and drunk sangria and posed for pictures in big, straw sombreros. The air had rippled with heat haze and the sound of cicadas and the smell of orange blossom and overflowing toilets.

Inevitably, there was a slick-haired waiter with butterscotch skin, courting them both and when Kiki caught them together on the sun lounger, there had been an almighty fuss. Rodrigo, or whatever-his-name-was, something with an 'o' anyway, insisted he didn't know they were twins. Or, rather, having no English, he'd made a pantomime of looking from one to the other, open-mouthed, and shrugging.

Still, that had been decades ago and she had barely given a thought to the man over the years. Whether Kiki remembered the incident, she couldn't be sure.

Judith finished dusting the ceilings and behind the radiators. Then she buffed the light switches and hoovered the blinds. Finally, she changed back into her own clothes ready to leave.

When she went through to the living room, Tony was on screen, explaining to a woman with very long nails that the revolutionary clothes brush would transform her lapels. Judith touched the screen and curtseyed, as she usually did, a kind of lucky ritual of her own, and stood for a moment, soaking him in.

"Bless 'im!" she sighed. "He's so caring. A real gentleman."

"Are you coming tomorrow, then?" Kiki demanded. Her mouth was full and there were crumbs down the front of her fleece, even though she had no appetite and took hours to hobble to the kitchen.

"I suppose I could always try and do it all myself if you've got better things to do, like *hair appointments...*" she went on.

Tony turned to the camera. "And the Lapsweep 100 can be yours for just ninedeen, ninedy-nine," he twinkled. "That's right, ladies. Look your best for *less than twendy pounds!*"

His eyes were soft puddles, overflowing with understanding. He seemed to be saying, 'It's OK, Judy. You an' me, we can see this through together. Do what you gotta do. I'm here for you'.

Judith took a deep breath. "Yes, of course I'll come," she nodded. "See you tomorrow."

The traffic wasn't so bad at that time of day and it only took her half-an-hour to get home, the roads fanning out, the gardens becoming greener as she drove. It had been years since Kiki had visited her down here. First it was the dust, then the dog hair she couldn't tolerate. Last time it had been something about the pot pourri in the downstairs toilet giving her a headache.

When Judith pulled up outside her house, she sat for a moment. The bushes in the front garden needed watering and the lawn was looking dry. Since Graham died, she often dreaded the silence when she opened the front door so she

101

was glad to hear the phone ring as she put the key in the lock.

It was that nice Mr Bunce, talking so loudly that she had to hold the receiver away from her ear. He had splendid news, he thundered. Terry – or rather Tony – had been tracked down and had agreed to grant her an audience. Could she come to the salon the following Thursday, say at about six in the evening?

When the call ended, Judith was shaking so much she almost dropped the receiver. She spent the next few days light-headed with anticipation, letting her sentences trail off into nothing, misplacing things, tripping over.

She said nothing to Kiki. Even so, the next day her sister noticed her absent-minded manner and peered at her like she was squinting through a letterbox. Judith explained that it was probably the new painkillers she was taking for her back. Thank the Lord, Thursday was the one day she wasn't round there so she wouldn't have to answer any awkward questions about where she was going.

When the day came, Judith got ready much too early. Her new hairstyle had grown out a fraction and there was now a thin stripe of grey through the yellow, like road markings in reverse, which she hoped no-one would notice. She fluffed a coating of bronzing powder on her normally waxy complexion and put on a turquoise and lilac beach dress even though it wasn't the weather for it and it exposed the rough, red goosebumps that made her upper arms look like lychee skin.

"What do you think?" she asked her husband's photo. "Will I do?" He didn't reply but then he'd never been one to say much.

Finally, at six o'clock on the dot, she pushed open the door to Hairs & Graces, insides swirling like a washing machine on full spin. The salon was like a warm, purple cave, dimly-lit and empty except for two figures lurking at the back.

"Ah! Welcome, Mrs Riddle!" Mr Bunce smiled, standing and coming towards her. "So glad you could make it. May I introduce my very good friend, Tony Prince?"

Another person stepped forward from the shadows. With his arms outstretched and shoes tapping on the lino, it looked as if he was about to launch himself into a spot of Greek dancing.

"Lovely to meet you," Tony said, kissing her on both cheeks. There was a gurgle in his voice like he needed to clear his throat. "But please, call me Terry."

He was giving off the smell of carbolic soap and his transatlantic twang had vanished and been replaced by a Midlands accent that made her think of cattle lowing.

He was also, Judith noted, as she looked down on the circle of smooth, hairless skin on top of his head, much smaller than he appeared on screen. More like a jockey than a TV presenter, really, and she felt self-consciously hefty in his arms. He, too, had dressed for sunnier climes in a ruffled shirt that revealed a chest the colour of Kiki's sideboard.

"Come and have a sit down, bab," he gestured.

Bunce dragged a third chair to where they were sitting and handed her a chipped mug containing something fizzy and alcoholic.

"Cheers!" he announced, clanking his own cup against hers.

Judith took a large gulp. There was so much she wanted to ask him. Did the Klariton 135-s *really* remove mud, red wine and curry from most fabrics and floor coverings or was it clever camera work? Had that jumped-up madam, Gabrielle De Villiers, who demonstrated the face creams, had Botox?

"Top bloke," Tony said, jerking his thumb in his friend's direction. "Should've seen his 'amlet."

"Come now!" Bunce responded. "You're making me blush!"

The two men launched into a conversation about Old Times. Bunce insisted that it was Tony who'd been the better actor, lamenting the fact that he'd so narrowly missed out on a part in a Midlands-based soap. Tony said, wheezing and spluttering at the memory of it, that he would never forget the time Bunce had played a transvestite lavatory attendant in that mime show.

"But it must be fun on the shopping channel?" Judith intervened. "All those products to try."

Tony rubbed his forehead. "Ooh, it's a lotta work. A lotta work," he fretted. "Those lights are bloomin' hot, for one thing. I smell like a wrestler's armpit at the end of a shift, pardon my French."

"But everyone seems so friendly…" Judith tried again.

Tony laughed in a despairing manner. "If only you knew!" he shook his head. "Sharks, the lot of 'em!"

He'd got hitched two years back, he said, to Beverley Ashcroft who'd made her name selling handbags and flamboyant scarves on a rival channel. All had been well until she'd started complaining about him leaving the toilet seat up, not putting the bins out. The kind of thing, he was sure, that a real lady like Judith would never make a fuss about, he said, winking at her.

But the final straw, he sighed, was when he discovered Beverley had been having an affair with Brett Firkin, the Australian oik who demonstrated power tools. Thought he was something special, he did, just because he had his own workbench. Tony had been devastated, absolutely devastated, he said. He'd been down the pub with the guy numerous times after work. Bought him a beer, too.

On and on he went with his melancholy mooing. Pay cuts. Longer hours. Johnnie-come-latelys after his job. His fallen arches that throbbed after a day at the studio. Judith didn't have to listen to the actual words he was saying, the tone was enough. She felt like an airbed with a slow puncture.

She saw herself reflected in the mirror on the far wall – orange-faced, yellow-haired, like a sponge puppet from a children's TV show, sagging into her chair, toes turned inwards. And most of all tired, so terribly tired.

Suddenly irritated, she stood up. The two men stopped talking. Bunce jumped and Tony looked up slowly, as if half asleep. There was someone she'd like Tony to meet, she announced. Someone who was a big fan. Would he, she wondered, nip round the corner with her? It wouldn't take very long.

Moments later they were walking in the direction of Kiki's flat. There was a faint drizzle like hairspray in the air and Judith shivered in her summer dress. Tony sang 'Copacabana' to himself, dancing a little rumba back and forth in his built-up, snakeskin shoes as he went. Two youths in baseball caps, sitting on a wall, stared at him as he danced past.

When they reached Corned Beef Mansions, Judith pressed the buzzer. Receiving no reply, she tried again. Surely Kiki was there? She couldn't go very far these days, after all. She went round the side and peered in through the living room window. The TV was on and a bald man in cycling shorts was on the screen, smiling at the camera, bending over to one side then the other while dance music reverberated around him.

"…and stretch, 2, 3, 4…" he urged.

Kiki was standing in the middle of the room wearing leggings and a bright pink sports bra. Her fuzzy, grey hair was held back by a sweat band and she was following his instructions with gusto.

She turned and saw Judith watching her, open-mouthed. The two women stared at each other with matching, pinprick eyes, like two startled chameleons, neither one moving, for quite some time. Then Judith turned, face set firm as cement, and marched back to the doorstep where Tony was waiting.

After a few moments Kiki opened the door a crack and peered through. Seeing Tony on the doorstep, she gasped and let it swing open.

"Oh my God! Oh my God! Tony Prince! It really is you, isn't it?" she trilled. "But what are you doing here? Why…?"

"In you go!" Judith instructed, nudging Tony forwards.

"Oh, er… sure," he muttered as he stumbled inside. "Nice to meet you…"

Judith remained outside. As the door slowly closed, she could still hear Kiki shrieking, "I can't believe it!" over and over again.

"Nice place you've got here," she heard him murmur. "My ex used to live somewhere very similar…"

Judith walked round the corner and sank down onto the low wall next to the recycling bins. Everything was still and quiet. Night was coming in and the damp air was collecting on her skin like a layer of condensation on a packet of frozen fish fingers. She remembered her husband and how he always used to put his jacket round her shoulders on chilly evenings.

After a few minutes, she stood up again and made her way back to the salon. Picking up her handbag from the floor where she'd left it, she marched out, saying nothing to Mr Bunce who was standing there, a puzzled look on his face. She wouldn't be back that way for a long, long time. Etienne de Something-or-Other could shove it.

106

Croydon Facelift

Yvonne had got talking to an old biddy at the bus stop once. "Running late again," she'd sighed, rolling her eyes Heavenwards.

The woman, a genteel-looking type with a brooch on her coat, had responded by comparing the bus service to her bowel problems. "Nothing happens for days and then, whoosh!" she explained, punching a frail fist in the air. "It all comes out in one go!"

Yvonne said nothing but she wondered if you could get a similar sort of thing with brains.

It wasn't that she didn't know what to say, exactly. It was more that she had some kind of valve up top. All her thoughts seemed to bank up and then come tumbling out of her mouth like an upturned bowl of alphabetti spaghetti, forming random words and sentences where the letters fell.

In the canteen at teabreak when they were all talking, she would listen till her ears ached and then blurt out a response, more often than not to something that had been said fifteen minutes earlier.

And when people made remarks, usually Phil and that spotty trainee from the warehouse, it could be days before she could think of a suitable comeback. Just recently, they'd started explaining jokes to her.

She found herself telling that hairdressing man all about it a few days later. What she really wanted, she told him, was to be quick off the mark, to put people in their place.

"Ah! The eternal quest for the elusive bon mot!" he agreed. "They call it 'l'esprit d'escalier', I believe. You think of exactly the right riposte only a tad too late, when you're leaving the building or waiting for the bus home. Happens to me all the—"

"Big on the French, aren't you?" Yvonne leapt in,

cutting him short. "Got a string of garlic round your neck or summing?"

"Touché!" Bunce conceded, eyes widening in surprise. "Dare I say, you seem to be getting the—"

"What's your name, then – Jean-Pierre?" she stumbled on, her breathing shallow and fast as if she were giving birth. She couldn't believe what was coming out of her own mouth.

Bunce clapped his hands together in slow applause. "First class!" he glinted, "Though your sense of timing perhaps needs a *little* work."

He tried to comb his fingers through her hair, which was greyish-brown like London clay and just as sticky, what with all the gel built up in it.

"And so to the task in hand," he went on. "What's it to be for Penge's very own Mae West?"

It had been such a relief when he'd released her Croydon facelift. Her top knot was pulled back so tightly, she almost heard her scalp creaking like the ropes on an ancient sail boat as the scrunchie was twanged off and her hair allowed to slowly slump over her eyes.

Yvonne had no idea, really couldn't say why she'd been wearing it that way for the past twenty-five years except that all the women she knew had the same style – hair scraped back into a ponytail, plastered to the scalp with oil or gel and worn with one, maybe two, sets of gold earrings that they'd bought from a catalogue.

It wasn't much different, she realised, to those tribes in the jungle. She'd seen a programme on the telly about it. With it being so humid, people didn't bother much with clothes and just covered their what-have-yous with a bit of shammy leather. But what they considered really stylish was wearing a kind of ashtray-shaped plate in their mouths to make their bottom lips jut forward. Probably been doing it for centuries without giving it a second thought.

Without hesitation she'd told Mr Bunce that she wanted an angular, black bob like people wore in the 1920s. She had a second-hand kimono top at home which she was sure would complement it, if she could only remember where she'd put it.

Now, however, standing in her bedroom, getting dressed in the early morning light and peering at herself in the mirror, she had to admit the new hairdo didn't look quite so stylish with the lime green overall and patterned tabard she had to wear for work.

The way the bob perched on top of her head reminded her of one of those medieval kings who went around with a bowl cut and a suit of armour – though maybe, it had to be said, a king who had had a few too many banquets. 'Strapping' was what her mother used to call her but she wasn't fat, she just had a big frame. Which king was he now? Didn't they dig him up in a car park recently? No matter, it would come to her later.

Still, maybe the cigarette holder she'd bought from the pound shop would help, she mused. She didn't smoke but wafting it gracefully to and fro with one hand might add to the air of sophistication she was hoping to convey.

Yvonne wasn't normally one to bother with make-up but she knew you couldn't really take on a hairdo like this and go 'au naturel' as Mr Bunce would say. She had a crimson lipstick somewhere which had come free with a magazine. She rummaged in a drawer and found it and, after wiping off the fluff, she daubed it on her mouth, going over the edges to try for the impression of a larger, fuller pout. It was a bit wonky and some of it smudged onto her teeth but it would do. She shrugged on her fleece jacket, fastened the Velcro on her size-eight trainers, picked up her handbag and set off.

The streets were busy at this time of day with people

travelling to work or school. But where more well-to-do areas had lots of important people in raincoats, clicking across the pavements in their smart shoes as they hurried to catch the train, Penge had school children milling around, swigging bottles of milkshake, and young men in shirts with yellowing armpits waiting for buses.

When she reached the High Street, some workmen were putting up scaffolding outside the carpet shop. As she passed by, someone called out, "Cheer up, love! It might never happen!"

You couldn't blame them. With the Croydon facelift gone, Yvonne's forehead had lowered several inches and now had the look of corrugated cardboard. Her eyebrows, pulled for decades into an expression of surprise, now hovered above her eyes in a kind of Stone Age ridge. She could understand why people might think she looked fed-up, though she preferred to think of it as world-weary and wise.

But still, who did they think they were, calling out like that? Turning, she yelled up at them, though there was a tremor in her voice, "What are you gonna do for a face when King Kong wants his arse back?"

Silence. She caught her breath. Had she *really* just said that? A lorry roared past. She noticed a small child on a tricycle battling towards her, zigzagging left and right.

And then whooping like a howler monkey from above her head. "That's you told, Mick!" a voice called. Mick, whoever he was, muttered something she couldn't hear.

Yvonne walked on, shoulders hunched, heart pounding, not daring to look back. Underneath her uniform her ribs heaved up and down in silent laughter.

Minutes later she arrived at the cut-price supermarket. It wasn't opening time yet and the security guard sat by the doorway to see off any chancers hoping to buy a breakfast can of super-strength cider. He looked up from his paper as she pushed through the turnstiles.

"Blimey! Had your hair done, Yvonne?" he gasped. "I didn't recognise you there for a moment!"

"That's my name, don't wear it out," she called, the words trailing behind her as she swaggered past a display of German biscuits.

She moved down an aisle flanked by freezers to the back of the shop. A group of women of different ages and heights, but all in green overalls with their hair scraped back, gathered at the customer service desk like a row of onions. There was a ripple down the line as they nudged each other.

Yvonne's confidence shrank a little but there was no going back now. Fumbling through her handbag for the cigarette holder, she found it and slotted it through her fingers, trailing it through the air in a figure of eight.

"Now is the winter of our discontent," she announced, pronouncing each word crisply and startling herself. Where had she dredged *that* up?

The women looked at each other.

"Everything alright?" said Bernadette, the oldest of the group and, as staff supervisor, the most senior. "I see you've had your hair done." She spoke slowly and placed a reassuring hand on Yvonne's forearm.

Sandra with the thick ankles, known to all as 'Sarnje', took it personally when people changed things without telling her and she glowered at Yvonne, shrinking back in distaste.

Chantelle, a beefy woman in her forties, put her hands on her hips and waggled her head from side to side as if warming up for a performance of the Funky Chicken. "You bin takin' dem antibiotic, Yvonne?" she demanded. "Dem can make you do strange tings."

Chantelle had reddish hair and had to be careful going out in the sun. She was always sucking her teeth and going on about 'rice and peas' but as far as Yvonne remembered, the woman came from Sidcup which was egg and chips country and nowhere near the Caribbean. A couple of years back, though, it was rumoured that she'd had a fling with a Jamaican taxi driver who'd eventually gone back to his wife.

"That why you talk in that ridiculous accent, then?" she shot back. "You on medication or summing?"

Chantelle's jaw dropped and her face flushed like she'd been slapped.

"Close your mouth, love, there's a forklift coming!" Yvonne went on, turning on her heel.

She marched off towards the staffroom, feeling the same hysteria bubbling up in her stomach that she'd had with the scaffolders. She knew the women would be talking about her but so what? It was better than being ignored.

Over the next few days, well-timed words flowed from her as never before. She told the spotty trainee, thanks for the offer but no, she would rather not have one of his biscuits in case she got foot and mouth.

When Phil sniggered at her new hair and called her 'Lurch' she said, "How about *this* for a lurch?" and jerked her hip to the side, bumping into him and sending him sprawling across the condiments aisle.

When a customer enquired whether they sold a particular brand of toilet paper, she replied that wiping your backside on furry animals was unhygienic and cruel.

Her cigarette holder was with her at all times and on one occasion, she caught Sarnje in the face, just missing her eye. "Don't worry," she quipped, "you've got another one on the other side."

It wasn't that Yvonne planned to say any of these

112

things, as such. She had no idea what was going to come out of her mouth from one moment to the next but she had to admit it was thrilling. It was like jumping out of a plane into freezing cold air without knowing whether the parachute was going to open.

At night, she would wake in the small hours, memories of conversations that took place years ago and things she should have said streaming through her mind like a magician pulling endless silk scarves from his pocket.

Usually she was kept awake by the muffled sounds of screeching cars, gunshots and music coming from the-man-downstairs' telly. Put up with it for years, she had, but since she'd had a word with him out by the bins, he'd kept the volume down.

The following Friday was staff training. Every few weeks the shop closed early and all employees assembled in the canteen to discuss sales figures or a new promotion on cooked meats, though in reality it was the free booze and broken biscuits that lured them there.

Yvonne changed out of her uniform in the toilets. She'd unearthed her kimono top at the bottom of the laundry basket and, though it was a bit creased, it looked good enough with her leggings. Taking an eyeliner from her fringed handbag, she peered at the mirror and drew a small, black dot above the corner of her mouth.

Satisfied with her reflection, she went upstairs to the canteen. Usually she lurked at the back, hoping she wouldn't be asked any awkward questions, but this time when she walked in, people shuffled their chairs to one side to make room for her to sit down.

"I feel like that geezer in the Bible, parting the waves," she chuckled, "only without the beard."

Thirty or forty people sat in a semi-circle of orange, plastic chairs under harsh, strip lighting. The air smelt of yesterday's sponge pudding and stale water. Raymond, the store manager, was sitting at the front of the room, clicking his biro on and off. Next to him, yellow hair falling over his collar, mullet-style, arms folded and staring into the middle distance like retail's answer to the Sphinx, was Stuart Murray, Regional Head of Marketing.

Yvonne had never spoken to Stuart though she had seen him many times. He had some kind of reputation though she wasn't sure what it was, exactly. People were in awe of him and whispered his name and raised their eyebrows when they talked about him, though maybe they were just afraid because he was the boss.

The last time he'd visited, Angie from accounts had been found crying in the toilets. Yvonne had tried more than once to find out what he'd done but people always rolled their eyes and said things like, "Honestly! Do I have to spell it out?" or "I'm saying nothing."

When everyone was seated, Raymond called for silence and welcomed Stuart to Penge once again. They would be discussing, he said, ways to improve customer service, as designated by Head Office, after which there would be drinks and snacks.

Stuart stood up slowly. "Welcome, one and all," he began, wearing the expression of a man who would be spending the next couple of hours filling out his tax return. "It's truly heart-warming to see so many familiar—"

He was interrupted when the door at the back of the room swung open with great force, banging into the wall behind. Chantelle hurtled in like someone about to halt a wedding ceremony at the eleventh hour. She was wearing an African print dress with a matching turban and several strings of beads round her neck. "Sorry," she panted, struggling to catch her breath, "me come as quick as I could! Dem buses, they no come a de right time!"

Phil and the spotty trainee were sitting near the back. Hearing her speak, they both exploded with laughter, rocking back and forth and slapping their knees. Chantelle slunk into her seat, ruddy-faced, lips quivering. Yvonne couldn't help feeling a tiny bit guilty. Since she'd challenged her on the authenticity of her accent, people guffawed every time the woman opened her mouth. She knew only too well what that felt like.

Stuart turned to a clean page on the flip chart next to him and drew a large, crescent shape with a squeaky, blue marker pen.

"Anyone know what that is?" he gestured.

In all her life Yvonne had never called out in a crowd – not at school nor in a meeting, not even at the panto where it was expected of you. But now, before she could stop herself, she bellowed, "Give us a clue, Leonardo!"

The room went completely silent. Raymond stopped clicking his pen and stared at her. Phil and the trainee turned to look, too. Neither of them was laughing. As for Stuart, he paused for just a second, acknowledging the outburst with the merest flicker of a frown, like a long-suffering dog ignoring the pesky flies buzzing around its muzzle on a hot day.

"It is, of course, a banana," he carried on, "or *is* it?"

He continued his presentation, making the point that employees shouldn't assume that their customers had the same level of knowledge and understanding of the merchandise that they themselves did. New products were arriving on the shelves all the time and all those present, he pointed out, should take the time to acquaint themselves with these things, all the better to advise the general public.

Yvonne wasn't really listening. She was thrilled, of course, that she had produced a wisecrack at just the right moment, rather than thinking of it two days later. Still, she was unsettled. Stuart hadn't responded at all and Phil, who creased up when anyone so much as opened a bag of crisps, had been stony-faced.

She remembered something her mother often used to say about her grandfather, a bingo caller and self-appointed 'life and soul', who'd been sacked for making inappropriate comments to customers. "He was a double-edged sword," she said, a warning tone to her voice. "You never knew which side you were going to get."

Yvonne tried to remember her grandfather, who'd eventually disappeared on a cruise liner amid stories that he'd shacked up with a Filipino woman half his age. But her daydreams were interrupted by the sound of people pushing their chairs back. The presentation was clearly over. Along with everyone else, she made her way to the drinks table and helped herself to a plastic cup of a cheap, Slovakian liqueur that had recently been introduced to the wines and spirits section. It tasted like nail varnish remover mixed with syrup and coconut ice.

Knocking it back in one, she was pouring another, when she heard a voice coming from behind. She turned and saw Stuart appraising her, his blue eyes expressionless. He had a little gold chain fastened across the collar of his striped shirt, she noticed, and a couple of cheap-looking gold rings on his fingers.

"Sorry – did you say summing?" she said.

"I said, I hadn't seen you here before," he repeated. There was a slight northern twang to his voice. "What's your name?"

"Yvonne's the name and drinking's my game," she replied, taking another glug of liqueur.

Stuart continued to stare and for a moment she wasn't sure whether he'd even heard her. Then he started making a heaving sound and she wondered whether he was about to throw up. Finally, as the sounds came closer together, she twigged that he was laughing.

"I'll have some of what you're having!" He chuckled and swiped the bottle of coconut liqueur from the table. He took a large mouthful and then another. "Blimey!" he went on, voice hoarse and eyes watering. "I didn't know we sold anything this good!"

Before Yvonne could reply, Angie from accounts toddled across and positioned herself between them. She was small with blue eyes and a turned-up nose. Her blonde hair was scraped back as always, with the resulting curly pony tail tumbling down her head like a fountain of spaghetti. Yvonne had always felt like a big, sullen rugby player in her presence, what with her chirpy manner and her tiny, high-heeled shoes.

"Stuart!" she trilled, ignoring Yvonne and throwing her arms round his neck. "We haven't seen you down here for a while. How's it going?"

"Not too bad," he answered, peeling her away from him as if something unpleasant were stuck to his lapel. All the while he was staring straight at Yvonne.

Yvonne flushed. There was a challenge in that stare, though she didn't know what it was. She moved away and collected herself a paper plate of crisps and sausage rolls. Phil came to join her with the trainee in tow, raising a can of beer in salutation.

"Go and look in the mirror before you start on my hair," she snapped. She noticed he was wearing a clean, white shirt which suited him a lot better than his usual boiler suit.

"What do you mean?" he answered, puffing his chest out and smoothing his thinning hair down.

"Just saying," she went on. "You ain't no oil painting, either."

117

"We're the same, you an' me," he added. "We like a laugh, don't we?"

Yvonne glanced behind and saw Stuart still staring at her. She flushed again.

"You want to watch him," Phil whispered, nodding in his direction. "Especially when he's had a drink. Know what I'm saying?"

For the rest of the evening Stuart continued to stare at Yvonne. When she was talking to someone, there he was, in her line of vision. When she came out of the toilets or poured herself another drink, he was there, too, saying nothing but making his presence known. She tried to avoid catching his eye but sometimes she couldn't help herself. With the bright colours of her kimono top and its loose sleeves, she was like a butterfly pinned to the spot by his gaze.

She wasn't used to receiving any kind of attention from men – well, not unless you counted being laughed at. Was it possible, she wondered, that he was flirting with her? It made her feel nervous but also important in a way she hadn't experienced before. Was this what her mother meant when she went on about being a 'femme fatale' in her youth?

Eventually the evening came to a close. The overhead lights were snapped back on and people started stacking the chairs into teetering orange towers. Yvonne had drunk more than she'd intended, moving from the coconut concoction to something banana-flavoured that was equally powerful, and she felt woozy.

She went to the toilets to pick up her coat and uniform and, when she came out again, Stuart was nowhere to be seen. Her brief experience of being a temptress appeared to be over and she was almost disappointed as she made her way downstairs, holding tightly to the handrail to stop herself falling.

Outside, she began to walk carefully across the almost-deserted car park in the direction of her flats. It had been raining and an oil slick floating on top of a puddle glistened like a rainbow under a street light.

A figure came towards her from behind a skip. "Fancy seeing you here," Stuart drawled, taking a mouthful from a bottle of red wine that she recognised as being on special offer in the store. "Want some?" he pushed it towards her.

Yvonne would have jumped if she hadn't been so drunk but, still, she was surprised. "No thanks," she answered. "I've probably had enough."

Before she knew it, Stuart was up close, breathing coconut fumes in her face. "But I've had nowhere near enough of you, my dear," he murmured. He swung his right arm round several times like he was bowling in a cricket match, bringing his hand to bear on her left buttock and squeezing hard. "…and there's plenty to go round, I see."

It took a moment for Yvonne to register what was happening. Was *this* what romance was all about? Where were the flowers? The kind words? One thing was certain – she had no intention of becoming a human stress ball for over-worked supermarket executives. Tears springing to her eyes, she put her hands on Stuart's shoulders and shoved, sending him sprawling backwards onto the tarmac.

He staggered to his feet, a smile creeping across his face. "Spirited, eh?" he leered. "I knew you had a bit of gumption!" He came towards her again, crouching low as if he was about to perform a martial arts manoeuvre.

But before he could get hold of her again, another figure loomed up from the shadows. The person grabbed Stuart round the waist and, grunting with the effort, hoisted him over his shoulder in a fireman's lift. Stuart was too drunk to resist but it didn't stop him yelling, "Put me down, you bloody clown!" as he was plonked into a stray shopping trolley that was standing nearby. The man shoved the trolley as hard as he could, sending it hurtling across the car park and into a bush on the far side where it tipped over.

"Alright?" said Phil, panting with exertion. "I told you to watch him, didn't I? Come on, Lurch," he went on, taking her hand. "Let's get you home."

Yvonne, still trying to process what had happened, was lost for words.

Suky

Suky undid the laces on her flat, brown brogues, slid them off and placed them side by side next to the wardrobe. Then she lay down on the bed, smoothing the pleats of her skirt flat and folding her long, translucent, tinned-asparagus fingers across her chest.

Above her in the sloping ceiling, the window revealed nothing but a rectangle of sky, heavy and white like it had been given a lick of emulsion. She felt calmed by its emptiness, like her little room, whose plain, white walls contained nothing but a bed, wardrobe and chair.

She took a deep breath and closed her eyes. It had been a challenging day.

That morning in the newsagent there had been a woman in front of her in the queue. She was in her thirties, short and trim with mid-brown hair clipped into a tidy helmet-shape like on a child's plastic, action figure. It was so clearly wrong for her. Surely anyone could see that she needed texture, a few layers, maybe some highlights? The floor had lurched beneath Suky's feet and she had to hurry outside for some fresh air.

Then, at lunchtime, when she'd nipped out for a sandwich, she was rummaging for the keys to let herself back into the salon when she heard a high-pitched, wailing sound behind her. She turned to see a toddler, a boy of about three, in a yellow rain mac, arching his back in protest as his mother strapped him into his pushchair.

As he thrashed around, kicking his wellies up and down, Suky caught a glimpse of his hair. A lopsided fringe sat high on his little forehead, the sides of his head were shaved while at the back, soft tresses fanned out down to his shoulders like he had a hairpiece clipped on. No wonder the poor little mite was screaming! It was all Suky could do to stop herself punching the woman in the jaw.

Eventually, though, she'd controlled her shaking hands enough to unlock the door and go inside for a chamomile tea.

Some people were sensitive to sound or colour or pungent smells. Others could tell what people were thinking just by looking at them. For Suky, though, it had always been hair. The sight of a bad perm or a wonky fringe could ruin her day.

Even as a young child she used to stare at people in shops, on trains and buses, imagining what they'd look like with short hair, long hair, perms, colours, layers. She didn't even have to think about it all that much – she just *knew* what was right for them.

Seeing the ridiculous hairdos Mr Bunce inflicted on his customers had been agony at times. When he'd turned that old lady's white hair into a divot of turf, bright green and spiky with artificial daisies woven into it, it was like a physical pain. He, on the other hand, looked mighty pleased with his efforts and so did the customer.

She'd found out how he was doing it soon enough but, the funny thing was, she couldn't condemn him. She understood where he was coming from. People really *did* need better hairstyles. He was just going about it the wrong way.

Now Mr Bunce was off somewhere, she could…

There was a tap on the bedroom door and two round eyes, sooty lashes surrounding them like wrought iron railings, peeped through the gap.

"Heavens above, Our Sooo-keh!" said a voice. "You look like one of them carvings on a tomb, lying there like that!"

Suky's Auntie Brenda came into the room, quivering like a guinea pig with nervous energy. She was the sort who liked to flap around and tidy up but finding there was nothing in there to fold up or put away, stood defeated in the middle of the room, fiddling instead with her bracelet.

"You alright, love?" she asked. "You're looking very pale."

"I always look pale," Suky murmured, adding, as she opened one eye, "I'll do your roots for you later, if you like."

Brenda ran her fingers through her hair. It needed cutting, too. Suky had persuaded her that a deep red would suit her and, sure enough, she'd been right.

Her niece was such a funny girl, all freckly and fragile where her sister's other children had the Rutherford black hair and were given to screeching and climbing on the furniture. Saturday afternoons round their place was like visiting a safari park.

But Suky had always been quiet and watchful, the one who made the beds and put the bins out. She was that different, Brenda had often wondered whether she was the result of an affair. Maybe, she speculated, her mother had been abducted and impregnated by aliens? Such things happened all the time in America, apparently. She'd read about it in magazines.

"Well, I'll leave you in peace, love," Brenda sighed. "Come down when you're ready and we can watch a bit of telly together."

Suky lay on the bed a little longer. Even after all these months, having her own room was still a luxury and she liked to just soak up the silence.

But it wasn't just ill-advised hairdos that were bothering her that evening.

On the way home, she'd taken a detour to the supermarket to buy some plain yogurt and rye bread. Her auntie was always offering to make her a fry-up in the mornings but Suky preferred clean flavours so she bought her own breakfast and got up a bit earlier to prepare it. Saying she'd already eaten was so much easier than risking Brenda getting mardy.

When she came out of the shop, she had been fiddling with her change when someone shoved past her, knocking her purchases to the floor and splattering the yogurt all over the pavement like some giant bird had opened its bowels.

Furious, Suky had bent to scoop up her shopping, glaring at the guilty party hurrying away from her as she did so. A long, scarlet coat with a black, furry collar. Heavy boots with chunky heels. Hair like golden syrup, trickling down the woman's back and – was it Suky's imagination – a carefully-arched eyebrow, peeking back over her shoulder, icily amused at what she'd done?

Suky felt every muscle in her body go rigid.

Janice Coppard!

Bolton's very own Bad Fairy. There was bound to be trouble wherever she turned up! But what was she doing down here in Penge of all places?

Suky hadn't clapped eyes on her in months, since she was last home, though funnily enough, she'd been thinking about her only the other day when Mr Bunce had washed her hair. But the memory of Janice's voice, all singsong and sneering, would never leave her. "It's like you've got Weetabix glued all over yer 'ead!" she'd said. "Do you 'ave it done at an 'airdresser's or does yer dad get the lawnmower out?"

Janice Coppard had been blessed with thick, saffron-coloured tresses that curled in all the right places and shone when they caught the light like a gilt frame round an old-fashioned painting. Her face wasn't much to write home about, mind. A bit heavy in the jaw and she tended to breathe with her mouth open, but her hair could be coaxed into all manner of elaborate styles. Suky half believed all the plaits and the scarves, the curls and hairclips the little hussy had worn over the years were just to taunt her.

She kept her eyes fixed on Janice's departing back, inwardly daring her to look round once more and receive the full force of her rage. But she didn't oblige. She kept right on walking, even had the brass neck to look jaunty, too, until eventually she faded from sight somewhere round the carpet shop.

Suky was shaken for quite a few days after the encounter. She started every time she saw a person wearing red and twice, she trailed someone up the road, lurking in doorways and behind hedges, convinced she was following Janice until she saw the person's face and realised she was wrong.

In the evenings, when she returned from the salon, she lay on her bed, washed-out, exhausted and almost camouflaged against the décor.

Auntie Brenda heated up tinned soup. "Come on, love. You've got to eat," she coaxed one evening, pushing a bowl of cock-a-leekie towards her.

Suky began pulling a slice of bread into pieces and dropping it into her soup.

"Do you think, maybe, you've been working at bit too hard lately?" Brenda went on. "Only, you've been running that place all on your own. And breathing in all those chemicals – well, it can't be good for you."

"I'm fine," Suky muttered. Talking about Janice Coppard would only give the girl space she didn't deserve and her auntie, she knew, would only tell her there were plenty more fish in the sea and that time was a great healer. "I saw someone from home the other day, that's all," she shrugged.

"What? All the way down here in Penge? Are you sure?" Brenda questioned.

125

It was a fair point. Could she really be one hundred per cent sure it was Janice who'd pushed her at the supermarket? Southerners were always rude and in a hurry, everyone knew that. It could have been anyone. And why would Janice be down here in the first place? Maybe Brenda was right and she had been working too hard.

"Hey, remember what you did to Our Louise's Barbie doll that time?" Brenda tittered, trying to distract her.

Suky remembered the nylon tufts all over the floor. "I told her it would grow back," she giggled.

The next day, the cloud had passed and she resolved to put Janice Coppard from her mind. She had a new life now and a job with prospects. Why let that common little cow rob her of that, too?

That evening she stayed late at work doing the accounts and ordering new stock. With the customers gone, it was warm and peaceful in the salon with the streetlights coming on outside and the evening air all misty and blue. Mr Bunce being away, she could imagine it was all hers.

The bell tinkled as the door opened. A handful of dry leaves seized the opportunity and scuttled in on the chilly breeze.

"Sorry, we're closed," Suky called, not raising her head.

A voice snapped, "It's alright, I'm not stopping."

Suky knew instantly who that voice belonged to. Her heart started pounding so hard under her overall she thought she might be sick.

She looked up. There she was, standing in the middle of the floor, hands on hips, like a ringmaster in her scarlet coat. Suky hoped she wasn't going to start waving chairs around.

"So this is where you 'ang out, is it?" Janice sneered, looking around. "They told me you were down 'ere. Not sure about the purple walls."

Suky was relieved to know she hadn't been cracking up

126

that day at the supermarket though it was another thing altogether to have the little trollop strutting into her salon. Janice's hair, she couldn't help noticing, was looking a bit straw-like these days. Probably been over-styled, knowing her. A deep conditioning treatment would put it right.

"What do you want, Janice?" she asked, making her voice as level as she could, though behind the desk she was scoring the pen into the appointments book with great force. "Only, I'm a bit busy."

She knew only too well what Janice wanted. She was after a scrap, same as always, but she wasn't going to get it. Not this time.

"Just curious, that's all," she answered, swaggering across the floor, boots clunking as she walked. "Your 'air's not changed much, then. Still rocking that 'chipboard vibe'."

Over the years, Suky had heard just about every insult going when it came to her hair and she didn't much care what people said any more. But there was something about the way Janice said things that made her want to scream. Still, she was determined not to react. Keep cool, say nothing and maybe she would sod off back up the M6.

"Like I say, I've got work to do. Did you want anything in particular?"

"Get you!" Janice cackled. "Think you're a bit better than everyone else, do you, just because you work in London?"

She plonked herself down in one of the chairs and started swivelling left and right. "I suppose you reckon Jaden will come running back, he'll be that impressed? Well, sorry, he won't!" she screeched again. "He's quite happy with what he's got. 'Ere. Take a look at this," she went on, pulling a gold chain from under her collar. "See that? It says 'JJ' on it. He gave it me last Christmas."

Suky could feel her own necklace under her overall burning against her skin like a branding iron. She leapt up and marched across the room. Years of wrestling with her brothers had made her stronger than she looked and quick to spot an advantage. Before Janice knew what was happening, she had her in a headlock. The other hand snatched up the clippers from a side table and switched them on so they were buzzing like an angry wasp.

"Bald on top, bowl cut round the sides, was it, Madam?" she hissed through clenched teeth.

"Oy! Gerroff me!" Janice shrieked, arms flailing. "What the bloody 'ell do you think you're doing?"

Suky plunged the clippers into Janice's thick, blonde curls, close to the roots. See how she liked people laughing at *her*! But immediately the device started snarling up the hair, making a revving noise, like that time she'd hoovered up one of her dad's socks. Suky switched it off and lifted it away only for the whole of Janice's scalp to come away, too. Suky stood staring at the hairdo swinging from the end of the blades. "But you're—"

Janice sat rigid, bald as a baby ostrich.

A silence fell that seemed to go on for a very long time. Then, her face turned pink and crumpled in on itself like a piece of half-chewed bubblegum.

"Of course I am, yer daft cow!" she sobbed, wiping her nose on her coat with a snurching noise. "It's all dropped out – me eyebrows, me eyelashes, even me sodding armpits! It's called, allo-pee-*eee-eee-eee*-sher," she wept, shoulders heaving.

She brushed her tears away with the back of her hand and sure enough, her supercilious eyebrows dissolved into a sooty smear.

"He left me, didn't he?" she whimpered on. "Course, it wasn't anything to do with me going bald was it? Goodness me, *no*! Now he's with *her*, that Zoe Bishop who works at the garden centre. She's got loads of hair. I bet you're dead glad, aren't yer?" she spat. "Got what I deserved!"

Suky wasn't sure what she felt. Moments earlier she'd been ready to turn Janice Coppard into Friar Tuck. Finding that Nature had got there first, she was somewhat defeated. She put the clippers down. "So why did you come here?"

"You're the only person who knows how I feel," Janice sniffed. "You know what it's like to lose 'im. And they said you'd become a hairdresser. I thought you might..."

Suky's indignation rose once again. She wanted to punch her to the floor and kick her out the front door but holding her nerve she said, "Well, I think I have something that might help you. Come with me."

She led her to the wash basins. She washed and conditioned Janice's scalp, which was rather like soaping a balloon, explaining that she was using an expensive, Californian preparation which had been scientifically proven to restore hair-growth. After that, she sat her under one of the dryers, telling her that the heat would help to activate the hair follicles.

Once the hot air was flowing, Suky nipped into the office and activated Mr Bunce's hypnotic CD.

"What's that noise?" Janice demanded.

"Oh that? That's just the radio," Suky replied. "Take no notice."

Soon Janice was snoozing, mouth hanging slack. Hairless, with black make-up striped across her face, she looked like a Martian or a member of an avant-garde, acrobatic troupe. When the CD had run its course, Suky turned the dryer off and shook her unwanted guest awake.

"Well then," she said, settling her rival in front of a mirror and arranging a fluffy, purple towel around her shoulders.

Janice looked at her reflection, head on one side. "I was thinking a touch of gold might look quite nice," she mused. "Jaden loves gold."

"We can do gold," Suky agreed, voice trembling as she tried not to laugh. "I reckon he'd really go for that. He likes the exotic look."

"Really?"

"Urban Tribal," Suky nodded. "He thinks it's cool."

She went to a drawer in the back office and took out a can of spray paint she'd used to decorate a couple of candle holders. A few squirts later, she'd covered Janice's entire scalp in gold enamel. She looked like a Christmas bauble or a brass doorknob.

"It's dead sophisticated," Janice sighed as she looked in the mirror, examining herself from all angles. "He won't be able to resist. I'm off home tomorrow and I'm going straight round to ask 'im to marry me, you know," she warned, picking up her coat. "Might even invite you to the wedding. See ya," she called as she clomped out into the night.

When the sound of Janice's footsteps had finally faded, Suky picked up the discarded wig and hung it on a nail that was poking out of the wall behind the till.

Still shaking, she turned to the mirror and examined her own reflection. The evening's events, she noticed, had put an unexpected glow in her cheeks. Her short, fuzzy hair, on the other hand, remained exactly as it always had been though, for some reason, it didn't look that bad. Some might even say it suited her.

Suky smiled and, as she did so, there was a new light dancing in her feline eyes.

Other Publications by Bridge House

Other Ways of Being

by Gill James

Other Ways of Being is a an anthology of stories that point us to other times, other histories, other worlds including those of our near futures, other sexualities and other genders.

Order from Amazon:

Paperback: ISBN 978-1-907335-67-9
eBook: ISBN 978-1-907335-68-6

Because Sometimes Something Extraordinary Happens

by Debz Hobbs-Wyatt

Seventeen short stories by Debz Hobbs-Wyatt from over a decade of competition wins and shortlistings. Featuring *Learning to Fly*, winner of the inaugural Bath Short Story Award; *Chutney*, shortlisted in the Commonwealth Short Story Prize, and *Pushcart* nominated, The Theory of Circles.

Meet a mixture of beguiling narrators, from seven-year-old Leonardo Renoir Hope trying to change the past so his dad doesn't die, and George and his carrot-growing friends on an east London allotment waiting for the world to end, to Amy Fisher who realises that her husband, after his sudden death, is not who she thinks he is… but who is the other Mrs Fisher? This one adds a touch of medical horror to the mix.

All of the stories are about ordinary people when extraordinary things happen to them.

Order from Amazon:

Paperback: ISBN 978-1-907335-69-3
eBook: ISBN 978-1-907335-70-9

The Power of Love

by Phyllis J. Burton

The stories in *THE POWER OF LOVE* are quite simply about LOVE of all kinds. If you like romance, then these short stories are written just for you as well. There is plenty of that! The huge clock on Waterloo station acts as catalyst for that. But the collection also shows us other sorts of love: family ties, enduring love, old love, forbidden love, mended love, children's love for their parents, parents' love for their children, a love for old buildings, and love between animals and humans.

"If you're looking for short stories to read then look no further. These are great reads from Phyllis. The stories are tender, loving and well-written. I'd recommend these stories to everyone." (*Amazon*)

Order from Amazon:

Paperback: ISBN 978-1-907335-72-3
eBook: ISBN 978-1-907335-73-0